C000224926

Blue Husbands

David,

Thanks for the
conversation and
best wishes,

Don Dickerson

Don Dickinson

Blue Husbands

The Porcupine's Quill

CANADIAN CATALOGUING IN PUBLICATION DATA

Dickinson, Donald Percy, 1947-
Blue husbands

ISBN 0-88984-123-3

1. Title.

PS8557.I324B5 1991   C813'.54   C91-093954-3
PR9199.3.D53B5 1991

Published by The Porcupine's Quill, Inc., 68 Main Street, Erin, Ontario NOB 1TO with financial assistance from The Canada Council and the Ontario Arts Council.

In the same, or different form, some of these stories were previously published in *Canadian Fiction Magazine, Fiddlehead Review, Wascana Review, Grain, Quarry, Journal of Canadian Fiction* and the *NeWest Review*.

Readied for the press by John Metcalf.
Copyedited by Doris Cowan.

Cover is after a sculpture by Tony Urquhart entitled *Tic Tac Toe*.

Printed and bound by The Porcupine's Quill.
The stock is Zephyr laid, and the type, Ehrhardt.

Fourth Printing, 1995.

Contents

For my wife, Chellie,
with love and admiration

Hogarth's Arrangement

CRUSHED BY A DIVORCE that left him rattling around an apartment festooned with hand-crayoned greeting cards sent by his estranged children, Hogarth for several weeks drank large amounts of Scotch and toyed with the idea of suicide. His ex-wife, a banker, had been beautiful, intelligent, and unfaithful, and whenever he thought of her in the arms of her Swiss lover – the two of them whispering mutual funds and international exchange rates – he felt the urge either to suck his thumb or hammer the walls with a chair. In retrospect it seemed inevitable that his wife should've outgrown him, but that she should've taken his two daughters – to Europe, he'd last heard – opened up holes in him where none had existed before. At the advertising agency where he worked, instead of writing his usual copy, he scribbled long lists of items such as razor blades, ropes, revolvers, and various brands of cleaning fluids. When at last he was found on a window ledge seven stories above the street, his superiors referred him to a company psychologist, a bluff, belligerently unorthodox man named Burdock who pointed out that suicide was a waste of insurance premiums.

'They never pay off on a diver,' Dr. Burdock advised him. Large and athletic, the psychologist sported a virile bald head and a handlebar moustache, which gave him the air of a retired sergeant-major whose parade-ground voice was meant to inspire confidence. 'Dive,' said Dr. Burdock, 'and your equity dives with you.'

Dr. Burdock's office was crowded with potted rubber trees, so that on each visit Hogarth had to slash his way through them to the couch, as if he were on safari. The psychologist prescribed sedatives, and showed his patient videotapes of poverty and natural disasters, a technique he called 'guerrilla therapy.'

'Guerrilla therapy puts your petty problems into global perspective,' he told Hogarth.

'I like the alliteration,' Hogarth admitted, 'but my petty problems look pretty big to me. Maybe I lack compassion.'

'Look at me when you speak,' the psychologist said. 'And come out from behind that plant.'

'If I could hug my kids once a week or so,' Hogarth offered, 'if I could be sure they were all right, I think things would start to fall into place for me.'

'Hey,' the doctor rubbed his bald head. 'Let's be frank. The kids are a ploy, a red herring. The flaw resides in you, Hogarth; let's blast that flaw the hell out of there.'

'I'm not sure I want to do any blasting.' Hogarth sipped from his hip flask and studied the rubber trees. He wished he were smaller, living under their leaves.

After two months of therapy, Hogarth found he was drinking more. 'I'm up to a bottle a day,' he confided. 'These films about starving kids have got me worried. They make me wonder if my own kids are eating okay. And the storms in the South Pacific scare the hell out of me because I can't be sure my kids aren't on a cruise somewhere. I don't even dare think about orphans or nuclear war. No, no,' he said. 'I don't want to dive any more, but I don't want to do much of anything else, either. I appreciate what you've done, but these sessions are costing me a bundle. I'd like to send my kids some presents, but I've had to move out of my apartment and I'm down to macaroni and cheese four days a week and I can't seem to get the hang of this global perspective thing.'

The psychologist pondered for several minutes. 'All right,' he said finally. 'Okay. I've got a strategy for this, something different.' He started to hum. Or at least Hogarth thought he started to hum. He couldn't be sure: lately he saw and heard things through a caramel-coloured haze. Right now, for instance, he watched Dr. Burdock turn the colour of peanut brittle, tug at his moustache, turn a somersault and swing among the rubber trees like a gymnast on the flying rings.

Hogarth could hear himself sweat.

Dr. Burdock cartwheeled into the chair behind his desk. 'The company pays me a retainer,' he panted, 'but this'll cost you extra. Two hundred bucks a session.'

Hogarth lifted his flask and swallowed big. 'I can't afford that.' He closed his eyes. When he opened them again, Burdock was standing on his head on the window sill.

'Look,' the psychologist said. 'I'm going out on a limb here. The association could have my ass for this, but what the hell. There are ethical considerations.'

'Ethics are okay with me,' Hogarth said. 'It's money that's the problem.'

Burdock flipped off the window sill and landed lightly on his feet. 'Okay. Fine. We'll work around that.' He brushed off his hands. 'We'll waive the usual – the couch sessions, the work-shops, the testing. We'll even skip the two weeks' orientation program. Why go retail when we can cut the frills? For a flat eight hundred, I'll send you right to the warehouse.'

'Eight hundred dollars?'

'Seven-fifty then – but I'm dying. Seven-fifty and you're kill-ing me.'

'Maybe I could squeeze that out of my bank card,' Hogarth said. He had a hard time following Burdock, who appeared to be whipping off some sort of handspring over the furniture. 'What else would I have to do?'

'Take this,' Burdock ordered, one-handedly pulling a busi-ness card from his breast pocket. 'This will get you into the warehouse. After that you're on your own.'

'Warehouse?' The card carried an address, but no phone number. 'But how will I ...'

'Whoa!' Burdock hollered, as he landed in the splits on the desk top. 'The card's in your hand. Let the warehouse boys take a crack at this. Friday night, nine o'clock. Oh, and take your passport.'

'Am I going somewhere?'

'We're all going somewhere,' Burdock said cryptically.

Hogarth reeled and tried to focus on the card in his hand. 'I'm – I'm not sure how you've convinced me to trust you.'

'I'm a professional, son,' Burdock wheezed. 'Pay my receptionist on the way out.'

THE WAREHOUSE was a low cinderblock building on a desolate road near the airport, and after Hogarth paid the cab driver and knocked on a side door he was rushed inside by a sweating bearded man in greasy green coveralls. 'You're late, so let's move,' the bearded man said as he snatched Hogarth's card. 'We're always up to our necks on Fridays.' He turned and led Hogarth through the warehouse, a miniature city of boxes stacked on wooden pallets. Whirring electric forklifts hurtled between the aisles at rush-hour speed, and one of them actually nudged Hogarth and sent him sprawling to the concrete floor.

'I broke my bottle,' he told the bearded man, who pulled him to his feet.

The bearded man tugged at Hogarth's arm. 'I'm crying you a river,' he said.

They hurried past several workers in green coveralls who frantically threw Styrofoam packing into wooden crates, while others nailed the lids shut. Now and then a jet roared by overhead, and it seemed to Hogarth that the ceiling rattled. Around a corner the bearded man pushed him into a tiny office that was cluttered with order forms and invoices. A few dilapidated travel posters were stapled to the walls: a castle on the Rhine, a Mexican beach, a koala bear chewing eucalyptus leaves.

'Sit down,' the bearded man said. He poked his head out the door. 'Sonia!'

A skinny, curly-haired person in green coveralls walked in. She went to a computer terminal and started to type furiously.

'This the last one of Burdock's?'

'Yeah.' The bearded man checked his clipboard. 'Drinker, divorced, two kids in Europe.'

Hogarth felt dizzy. 'Isn't that privileged information?' he wondered. 'Look –' he tried to stand up, but found he couldn't. 'I feel dizzy, I must've bumped my head on something. Do you have any Scotch?'

Sonia looked at the bearded man and they both laughed. 'God I love these guys,' Sonia said. 'Call me crazy, but I love these seven-hundred-buck specials.'

'I paid seven-fifty.'

'Oh ho,' Sonia said, leaving the computer. 'The late flight. Here, have a drink.' She handed him a glass of something and Hogarth gulped it down.

'What late flight?' he said – or thought he did. There was no caramel-coloured haze this time, but he certainly felt dizzy. The bearded man seemed to be going through his pockets, and wasn't Sonia rolling up his sleeve? Wasn't that a hypodermic syringe she was poking into his arm?

'Is that a needle?' Hogarth asked.

'Questions, questions,' Sonia said. 'God, I love these guys.'

Hogarth drifted in his chair. The room bobbed up and down, and when he looked at his arm he found it'd become an oar. He was in a life-raft at sea. 'Holy cow,' he said. 'I sure hope none of those storms comes this way.' Something – a wave perhaps – picked up his life-raft and pushed it gently forward. A piece of seaweed drifted by his face.

'I don't see why we check them through on Friday nights,' the seaweed said. 'We're always up to our necks on Fridays. We're stacked up on the runways on Fridays.'

'It's all those specials,' a second voice said.

'There's too many of them all right.' The seaweed's voice was shot through with bubbles.

'Lift his feet,' the other voice said faintly. 'That's it. Don't you just love these guys?'

A thin wall of green water rose in front of Hogarth's eyes. It's like looking through leaves, he thought, before he felt himself being hoisted into the sky.

WHEN THE PLANE LANDED in London, the rain was falling like a beaded curtain, but Hogarth didn't notice. In fact, he couldn't remember disembarking or going through customs.

'I guess I'm just wound up,' he told the driver of the delivery van. 'The last time I was in London was fourteen years ago with my wife, on our honeymoon. It's quite a coincidence to be back here after all these years. I don't know why, but I feel really rested, and being back in London brings back happy memories.'

The van driver grunted and shoved some clothes at him. 'We're running a bit behind, mate,' he said. 'You'll 'ave ter change in the back as we go along.' The driver was squat-muscled and wore a cloth cap and a navy pea jacket, which fitted him snugly in the shoulders. 'And don't drop them little Styrofoam fings all over the carpet,' he said as he started the engine. 'I don't know what it is wiv you specials, you're always leaving them little Styrofoam fings layin' about.'

The van sped through the red-roofed suburbs and into the city proper. Through the narrow window in the back, Hogarth saw the grey wet streets and the sluggish waters of the Thames. Hunched over the wheel, the driver careered through narrow streets of grim apartment blocks, where dustbins leaned sadly in the rain, above the graffiti-slashed stone walls. ANARCHY RULES, Hogarth read. The raincoat he put on was tattered and smelled of mildew and rubber-tree leaves.

'Another coincidence,' he told the driver. 'The rubber tree smell, I mean.'

'Bit of a bump, 'ere,' the driver said. ''Ang on.' He wrestled the van around a sharp turn and geared down for a hill. 'Nigel will wonder where we've got to,' he said. At the top of the hill he stopped, rushed to the rear of the van and flung open the doors. 'Right, mate, out, out. I 'aven't got all day. You're not my only delivery, you know. Bleedin' late flights,' he said.

Stumbling onto a cobbled square, Hogarth squinted in the rain. He recognized the low, stolid outline of the Tower of London, and the span of Tower Bridge beyond. In front of him, on the puddled cobblestones, a sharp-faced man with no legs sat on a tin trunk.

'This is Nigel,' the driver said. 'Nigel, this one's the special – the divorced drinker wiv the two kids.'

''E's late,' Nigel said. His trousers had been shortened and stitched over the stumps of his legs. "Ow's he going to learn it proper? 'E don't know nuffing about it.'

The driver jumped back into the van. 'Come off it, Nigel – do your usual.' To Hogarth he said: 'You'll be all right wiv Nigel. Just don't say nuffing about 'is legs.'

'Wait a minute,' Hogarth said. 'Is this part of the deal?' He pointed at Nigel. 'He looks familiar. Didn't he used to have one leg, fourteen years ago?'

'I wouldn't know mate.' The driver threw in the clutch and madly shifted gears. 'I'll be along to collect you when it's over.'

'When what's over?' Hogarth wanted to know. But the driver waved and roared off.

The legless man had scooted off the tin trunk. He rode a little platform on wheels, like a skateboard. 'The buses stop 'ere,' he said, 'so we'd best get a move on before they come.'

'Hey,' Hogarth said. 'I remember now. You used to have one leg, and you wrapped yourself up in a burlap bag and lots of rope, and you tried to escape from it. And there was another guy here – what did he do? – I remember now. He was a chain-swallower, that was it. A tall guy with a beard in a ratty old raincoat. Helen – that's my wife, well, my ex-wife actually – gave you guys a ten-pound note. She cried that night, did you know that? She thought you guys must be terribly poor. Do you remember her? Slim, brunette, good legs and a smoky kind of look in her eyes –'

'You specials,' Nigel said disgustedly. 'I don't know why I bovver, really I don't.' He was busy unpacking the trunk, carefully laying out a burlap bag, coils of rope, and twenty feet of steel-linked chain.

'Holy cow,' Hogarth said. 'This is great. The same act with the burlap bag and everything. God, this brings back a lot of memories.' Memories flooded Hogarth's mind so quickly he had to rub his forehead. 'For instance, after we watched you guys fourteen years ago, I took Helen to St. Paul's Cathedral and we whispered to each other around the dome. God, I thought I'd forgotten this. Helen stood on one side of the dome and I on the other and we whispered how we loved each other and how we'd be true to each other even if we had only one leg and had to make a living escaping from burlap bags. And then on the way out Helen got her shoes wet so I carried her to the tube station, down the escalator and everything. And later that night we made love and – I can't be certain about this of course – but I think our eldest daughter was conceived in a bed-and-breakfast on Earl's Court Road.'

Nigel skateboarded around Hogarth's feet, spreading out the burlap bag. 'Let's get on it wiv it, mate,' he said. ''And us that chain, will yer?'

'Yeah, sure.' Hogarth wiped his face with his sleeve. 'Everything sort of started here with your act,' he went on. 'Of course the chain-swallowing was the big finale. No offence, but that guy who did the chain-swallowing number really got the crowd going.'

'I know all about it,' Nigel said. 'Tall bloke wiv a beard and a tattered mac – right?'

'That's right.' Hogarth looked down at himself: the raincoat he wore was tattered. He rubbed his bristled chin. 'Hey, I get it,' he said slowly. He was really sweating now. 'I get it. We're doing some sort of rerun here, aren't we? That's okay, I can go along with that. All I need is a drink, okay?' He felt thirsty all of a sudden. 'Sure, maybe a double, and we'll jump right into this.'

'You specials,' Nigel said. 'Always going on about your bottles or your needles or your pills. Well, I've got news for you, mate. If you want to see your two kids proper, you've got to see them just the way a bloke in a tattered mac would. And that means swallowing the bleedin' chain. No drinks, no nuffing. Just the chain. That's the arrangement, see. Look at yourself, mate. You're a stranger then, aren't you? You're just a bloke in a tattered mac, that's all. That's the arrangement. Now, now, don't start. All the blubbering in the world won't change fings, will it then? – There, that's better.'

Nigel picked up the chain and dangled it above his own mouth. 'Now, the trick is to open your froat up and keep it that way. You want to control what we call your gag reflex. Otherwise you'll frow up, and that puts your audience off. 'Ere, you give it a go. That's it, tip your 'ead back, and let it slide straight down, like spaghetti. That's the ticket. You'll do all right.'

'Something's happening here,' Hogarth said. 'I can see you and hear you clearly enough but I feel kind of shaky.' The chain he held rattled uncontrollably.

'That's just nerves, that is.' Nigel lifted his sharp face and listened as the first growl of engines echoed along the sidestreets. ''Ere come the buses,' he said.

TO HOGARTH his daughters looked exceptionally healthy and mature, poised as they were under their umbrellas, in the crowd of tourists that included a horde of noisy uniformed schoolchildren and a knot of Japanese businessmen, in surgical masks for the cold. No hunger had shrunk his daughters' cheeks, no tragedy had scarred their foreheads or twisted their limbs. From what he could see – as he lowered the chain link by link into his stomach – his daughters had adjusted to their new lives much better than he had. Charlene, his eldest, now wore eye makeup, and laughed delightedly when he shook himself to settle the chilly chain in his innards. Emily, the youngest, smiled shyly, her teeth a testament to several years of orthodontics.

'Of course, I'm just talking about superficialities here,' Hogarth told Dr. Burdock later. 'I mean what've mascara and no cavities got to do with anything? You have to look inside, don't you? God, I can't believe how cliché it sounds, but you know what I mean. Kids are pretty resilient, aren't they? Holy cow, another cliché. Well, it doesn't matter. The point is I got the whole chain down, I mean all the way down, because that was the arrangement after all, wasn't it? And when I turned to bow to the crowd while Nigel scooted around with his hat to collect the money, guess what I saw? Well, you probably already know this, but I saw Helen and the Swiss guy sharing an umbrella. She still looked beautiful and everything, but they were sharing an umbrella and my two girls were standing close to them, all of them laughing and then Charlene and Emily pestered the Swiss guy – their father, I guess you'd call him, and he dug into his pocket for a ten-pound note to put in Nigel's hat. That's pretty significant, I guess, but that's not the point. The real point is the way they pestered him made me think they were the kind of family that would probably visit St. Paul's Cathedral and whisper to each other around the dome. That's the kind of family they looked like to me.

'Hey, didn't you used to have a lot of rubber trees in here?'

Carapace

ON A GLARING STRETCH of sun-bright tropical beach swept by south winds and ribbed with dunes, McArdle, recently widowed, stumbled into conversation with a fiddler crab.

'But don't get any ideas,' the crab said. 'This isn't a fish story.'

'I'm not sure what this is,' McArdle said.

'I mean with the fish story you've got your dissatisfaction and your three wishes and the mythology and all that stuff, but we're not going to bother with that. Essentially what we're dealing with here is your basic talking crab.'

McArdle turned his back on the crab for a few moments and pinched the bridge of his nose between his thumb and forefinger. A landscape gardener by trade, he was a square, firm-bodied man nudging fifty-five whose wife had died of cancer the year before. The holiday in the tropics had been his wife's idea; they were to have gone together. She'd bought him a straw hat and herself a bikini, and in the hospital she'd whispered to him from a cloud of pain and sedatives, 'Oh, look at the porpoises.' His eyes were open, so he couldn't see what she saw. 'And the coral,' she'd said, 'and the white, white sand. Ah,' she'd wept. 'The water's so warm here.'

Still with his back turned, McArdle lifted his straw hat and ran a hand over his thinning hair. He shook his head. 'I've heard about things like this,' he said, and started to walk.

'Hey!' The crab scuttled in the sand. 'Hold on. Where are you going?'

McArdle strode away under the sky. The air smelled of heat. The beach was a vast Sahara, burnt white along the hills where ragged tufts of grass pushed up through the sand: a beach deserted, as naked as the sky, except for a few stunted eucalyptus trees, which, stripped of bark, bared limbs as smooth as bone. As he walked, McArdle squinted: no surfers rode the waves this morning, though the combers rolled in perfectly. Turquoise and translucent, the Pacific rhythmically reared up and folded in on itself, hissed down long glass troughs and ran sheets of boiling foam landward, where McArdle's footprints dissolved in the sand.

'Slow down, can't you?' The crab panted behind him, his voice pitched above the roar of the surf. 'Christ, are you trying to kill me?'

'I'm used to laying lawn sod and planting a few shrubs,' McArdle said. 'I'm not used to this kind of thing. I'm just here on holiday.' He sat down to look out over the ocean, screwed his heels into the sand.

'That's better.' The crab scrambled to hunch beside him, wheezing, resting his enormous claw in front of him. 'Relax. Take it easy.'

The tide drew back, leaving a wet strip as broad and smooth as a highway. Where the sea touched the land, the sand was stained the dark colour of clay, packed like wet cement. Out on the headland where the red rocks jutted into the water, the spume kicked skyward. McArdle watched the spume and leapt with it, wincing when it collapsed on the rocks.

On the beach around him other fiddler crabs popped out of sand holes like miniature armoured tanks. They waved their oversized claws above their heads like mad violinists and scuttled in and out of the tide pools, grubbing with their other, atrophied pincers in the muddy sand.

'Pound-of-fleshers,' McArdle's crab said. He was bigger than the others, heftier, a rust-coloured carapace. His small, glittering eyes shifted on their stalks.

'They have to live, I suppose,' McArdle said.

'You got that right.' The crab settled in the sand. 'I prefer to eat early in the day. More variety then, know what I mean?'

McArdle watched the ocean rise and fall along the horizon. He remembered his wife's ruined chest fluttering under the hospital bedclothes. A sudden breeze lifted his hat from his head, sent it skittering away from him, rolling on its brim.

The crab scuttled sideways, lashed out and returned with the hat clamped in its oversized claw.

'Thank you,' McArdle said.

'No problem. Broke a few strands, though.'

McArdle regarded the crushed brim. 'You move pretty fast, for a big fella.'

The crab resumed his position and stared out over the ocean.

'I'm here to help,' he said. 'I aim to please.'

AT NIGHT in his rented caravan, McArdle wrote postcards he would never mail, to his wife who would never read them.

Warmer here than we ever imagined, he wrote. *Air like a bath. At night the fruit bats feed in the mango trees. Locals call them flying foxes.*

He wrote: *Sun drops into ocean at six p.m. Tonight saw the Southern Cross for the first time. Just like the Aussie flag. The Milky Way a definite white splash, not like at home. A smear of snowflakes over a black roof.*

He wrote: *Have seen many animals here, birds. Kangaroos of course. Also cockatoos, parakeets, tree frogs, snakes, dolphins. Fiddler crabs. Also a noisy cicada that looks like a bubble with leaves for wings.*

Kookaburras get up with the sun. They really have that laugh.

Goddamnit, Alice, he wrote. *You're supposed to be here.*

THE WEEKENDERS started to arrive on Friday afternoon: couples with children, couples without children, long-haired surfers trailing surf boards and girlfriends, teenagers carrying ghetto blasters; men in shorts, older than McArdle, tanned and stringy-muscled, fishing gear slung over their shoulders.

'You're moping,' the crab said.

'I'm just watching.'

'Get in there and mix, what the hell.'

'I'm okay.'

Umbrellas went up, coolers were set in the shade, sun block was dabbed on noses. Kids scampered shouting into the foam. A lifeguard's yellow jeep roared through the sand. A thin man set up a camera with a two-foot lens on a tripod and aimed it like a gun at the surfers cresting the waves.

'All right,' the crab said. 'That's it. I got to break a rule here.'

'What rule?'

'Never mind. I got rules, all right?' The crab hunkered down, pivoting to eye a crowd of squealing kids charging the surf with pails and sand shovels. 'I got to make it fast, though. See those little bastards?'

'They're just kids.'

'You got kids?'

'No.'

'Then don't talk to me about kids, okay?' The crab began to worm himself into the sand, a sideways shuffle. 'Jesus, one of them's got a metal sandpail,' he said.

McArdle leaned back on his elbows. 'You were going to break a rule.'

The crab had nearly buried himself. The top of his carapace glinted flatly in the sun. 'Try the headland beach.'

'It's all rocks.'

'It's not *all* rocks.'

'There's nothing there.'

'You been there?'

'I've looked.'

'But have you been there?'

'No.'

'All right then. Try the headland beach.'

Three tow-headed youngsters sprinted past, their heels spitting sand.

'I'm under,' the crab said, muffled. 'I'm gone.'

PUBIC HAIR – a tufted wisp tinged red by the inevitable sun and set astir, like moss, by an offshore breeze – beckoned McArdle from behind the rock he'd chosen to sit on. Confronted unexpectedly by the woman's nudity, he sought to look elsewhere – sought, in fact, to slide behind the rock and slink away, seared by the image of large, shapely thighs and bronzed, heavy-nippled breasts.

'Excuse me,' the woman said.

Embarrassment stopped McArdle in his tracks but wouldn't allow him to emerge from behind the rock. Promising himself not to linger on the fine points of anatomy, he looked instead directly into the face of a large, naked woman whose startling eyes were pale, unburdened, the green of new grass.

'I'm sorry,' McArdle said, a bit surprised that he actually was. 'I didn't mean to spy on you. I was out walking.'

'You're on the nudie beach, you know.' The woman's voice carried a faint, side-of-the-mouth Australian twang.

'I didn't know.' McArdle took off his hat and mopped his forehead. Despite the safety of the rock, it was he who felt exposed.

'Oh,' the woman said. 'I thought it might be you.'

He recognized her then as the woman in the caravan up the hill from his. She was an artist – or at least she painted. One evening he'd seen her seated in front of an easel under her trailer's awning. She'd been wearing a flowered dress of indeterminate shape and her hair, thick and lank, had been plaited along her neck. Sneaking a glance, he found it difficult to reconcile this rich brown expansive flesh with the person whom, after all, he'd scarcely noticed.

'Not painting today?'

'Not at this hour. I'm after the evening light.' She raised herself up on her elbows so her somewhat elongated, ponderous breasts plumped on either side of her oiled chest. She studied him for a moment. 'If you promise not to blink,' she teased him, 'I'll invite you to sit down.'

He apologized again, stumbled out from behind the rock and perched on the edge of her blanket. She reached into the cooler behind her and handed him a can of beer. He caught a whiff of suntan oil and perspiration, not unpleasant. Though younger than he, she was not young. Grey streaked her dark hair, stretch marks creased her belly.

'Who do you talk to?' she asked.

'Pardon me?'

'I've seen you, along the beach in the early morning. Who are you talking to?'

'No one.'

She laughed – a deep, fruity sound that made him turn to her.

'Come on, then,' she insisted. 'No secrets here. Who are you talking to?'

He sipped his beer. 'A crab. A fiddler crab, actually.'

'Ah,' she said. 'A crab. Not Goorialla, then?'

'Who's Goorialla?'

She lay on her side, hip-jutted, her smooth brown belly rounded like a swag. 'The great rainbow serpent. The aboriginals believe he lives in the sea. I'm trying to paint him. He's a bit shy, though – only shows himself to me as the sun goes down. He hasn't spoken to me yet, but I always hope.' She tipped her head back to swallow a mouthful of beer. 'So what's he talk about, your crab?'

'Nothing.'

'Go on. I've heard you rattling on. What's he say?'

'Nothing much. You know crabs. They're not great conversationalists.'

She smiled at this. 'I reckon I know *that* sort,' she said. 'I was married to one once.' She swallowed again. He watched her broad throat working.

'You haven't blinked yet,' she said.

'Give me time.'

'That's one of the reasons I come here,' she said. 'It gives me time.'

They sat for a while, drinking. The sun moved. Above them, among the red-trunked eucalyptus and fuzzy-headed black-boy palms, bell birds tinkled like fine silver.

'You stay up nights as well,' she said. 'I've seen your light. You're writing. What do you write?'

'Postcards, letters.'

The beer seemed to have gone to his head, or perhaps it was the sun. Languid, bilious, he lay beside her, hands behind his head. The sky spun over the treetops, shadows slid away from the rocks, words welled up into his throat. He talked of his wife, of her months in hospital, of her breasts which had been removed – uselessly, as it turned out. His wife hadn't so much died, as dwindled, as if the disease had only wanted to make less and less of her.

Oh, Alice, he thought.

He unbuttoned his shirt, lay in the stale late afternoon heat, while around him the cicadas began their incessant sawing. Beyond his sandalled feet, beyond the rocks, the tide crept up the sand to lap the shore in sleep cadence. Naked in her listening, the woman anchored him to this strange shore. She handed him other beers while he talked on. The heat lay on his words, undiminished. He closed his eyes. His voice drifted among the rocky outcrops, reached tenderly under his wife's fragile body and lifted her, as light as the tinkled song of bell-birds, into the lukewarm sea.

In the lengthening shadows, the cicadas sawed through his words, and fell silent.

The woman drew him warmly to her, gathered him without lust into her arms.

Thinking of her as the sun, he slept.

'YOU DID WHAT?' the crab said.

'I fell asleep.'

'You fell asleep. I broke a rule, and you fell asleep. She was naked, wasn't she?'

'It wasn't like that.'

'You could've taken your clothes off.' The crab grew agitated. In the fading light his rust-coloured carapace took on the menacing shade of dried blood. He reared back in the sand, lifting his oversized claw above his head. 'That tears it,' he told McArdle. 'I'm out of here.'

'What do you mean? What's the matter?' McArdle stood with his back to the sea. Against the shore's gloom he could barely make out the crab who was shuffling to his right.

'This was a one-shot deal,' the crab said. 'I lined you up, I broke a rule, and all you did was fall asleep.'

'What would you have done?'

'I'm a scavenger,' the crab hissed. 'We grab what we can.' He scuttled back and forth, claw waving.

'Let's talk,' McArdle said.

'Talk's cheap,' the crab said. 'Get out of the way.'

McArdle approached, extending his hat towards the oversized claw, but the crab ducked the invitation, preferring to hoof it to the ocean. Scampering, McArdle headed him off. Instead of retreating, the crab squared himself for a last stand. McArdle extended the hat again, and in a single clack of pincers the crab clamped the brim in his claw. McArdle tugged a little, the crab tugged back; locked together, they pulled. The crab's claw gave way at the shoulder, tore, parted. McArdle flopped backwards in the sand, the hat – with the severed claw embedded – still in his hand.

'Oh, God,' he said. 'I'm sorry.'

'Bastard,' the crab grunted. He scurried around McArdle into the white line of roiling surf.

In the darkness McArdle fingered his torn hat and the powerful jaws of the pincers. 'Hey,' he called when he thought of it, 'hey, don't these things grow back again – don't they regenerate?'

But the crab had disappeared. And though he listened, all McArdle heard was the sound of his own breathing, and the sea crashing in windy booms, like an exuberant forest opening to a northern gale.

The Accident Business

SEPTEMBER 3: The day nurse who relieves Miss Shinkel at eight a.m. is named Mrs Arnold. A fat, intimidating woman whose chin has disappeared into her neck, Mrs Arnold isn't nearly as attractive as Miss Shinkel is. Mrs Arnold is sixty-one years old and sensible. Miss Shinkel is twenty-two and va-voom. The difference between them is obvious, and for some reason it should be significant to me. I'm not sure why. Either there's something at work here that I've forgotten, or I never knew it in the first place. I can't be certain. I could blame this confusion on senility, but I don't think it's that. I'm eight-four. The way this arthritis is going, I don't think I'll make it to senility.

You'd think Mrs Arnold would be more sympathetic towards Emily and me, being somewhat closer to us in age. She isn't. And looking ahead, she probably won't be, either. Whenever I hear her bark orders further down the hall, I realize Mrs Arnold must see in Emily and me – maybe in all of us here – a preview of her worst fears for herself: farty old apples, dropped from the tree and piled up here in the Sunset Home for Pioneers. And from the way she pounds her heels into the hallway tiles, my guess is that Mrs Arnold is a fool for the military. No, above all else, Emily and I will have to keep this escape plan secret from Mrs Arnold.

'Morning, Mr Hurd.' Mrs Arnold's greeting is an announcement. She has her clipboard tucked under one massive arm and accepts my good morning without even a nod. She waits. She doesn't see my notebook, which I've slid under the quilt. I hunch down into my pillow, and position her florid face between the two gunsights of my feet, which lump the end of the bed.

'How is old Tim?' I ask, as a test.

'Poor Mr Ecklestone is no longer with us.' Mrs Arnold glances at the trapped clipboard, as if he's there. 'He passed away quietly during the night, I'm afraid.'

So. She's still at it. Her grey eyes meet mine and hold there; not like the reddened eyes of Miss Shinkel, who genuinely liked old Tim, and who was as upset as we were to hear him rage and whine like that at the end. Miss Shinkel had to give him a sedative. But I'm not about to contradict Mrs Arnold's image of a sad-but-tasteful death, because she's pasted professional resignation on her face. I nod and smile wistfully, partly in honour of old Tim, and partly because I've learned from other deaths how final Mrs Arnold's resignation can be.

Tim Ecklestone is never to be mentioned again.

SEPTEMBER 4: There are rules to live by. They are listed in columns. Emily, I am told, is confined to her room in the women's wing, and I am prohibited from visiting her. 'She needs rest,' Mrs Arnold tells me. For Mrs Arnold, rest is one way to keep shaky widows and widowers in proper perspective; at opposite ends of the building. Illness is another. When I groan, she raises one well-plucked eyebrow. 'Arthritis, Mr Hurd?'

'Yes.' I lie, hoping to confound her. For her benefit I wear my full eighty-four years. I clutch the arms of my chair, yawn, and clack my dentures. I listen to the ticking clock and muffled coughs and snuffles that come from the other rooms. 'Old Tim never had arthritis,' I say. Letting it slip. Mrs Arnold stares at me, so I have to improvise some slobbering and dithering. I work at getting old and tired. Finally she leaves: her rubber-soled shoes squeege sceptically down the hall.

I'm not sure why I make these blunders. It should be easy for me to feel old and tired. The quiet in here is an old and tired quiet. We're kept amused by old and tired things: faded checker-boards, dominoes, and last year's *Reader's Digest*. At two o'clock the TV will go on, in time for the soap operas. Afterwards there'll be tea, and later the news, and then supper, and so on, and on. As predictable as the markings on a yardstick. Most of us here know we're sliding along towards the inevitable THE END, bowling balls headed straight down the gutter. They have no room for the accident business in here, no room at all. They'll nudge us along to THE END, so that like all the other old geezers here before us we'll drop out of sight, off the list, down the tube.

It has something to do with lines. There's something linear in all of this. Eighty-five comes after eighty-four, tea comes after the soap operas, Mrs Arnold checks one room after another, like beads on an abacus wire.

After Tim Ecklestone comes silence.

It has something to do with straight lines.

SEPTEMBER 5: Emily is still in her room. She has, thankfully, nothing more serious than constipation. Miss Shinkel tells me this. Miss Shinkel is young enough to appreciate the love-gaze collision. When it happened to Emily and me, I tell her, it was an accident of the Order One. Miss Shinkel laughs delightedly, and shows me a dentist's dream.

Later, I watch Miss Shinkel and Mrs Arnold near the nurses' station as they exchange the reins of responsibility. The contrast is almost overwhelming. Just as one trots her vivacious youth and cheerful bottom out the glass doors, the other marches earnestly down the hall to test our deafness and gag us with vitamin pills.

Willy-nilly, fortune has meted out unequal portions of practicality and pizazz.

SEPTEMBER 6: I wonder about the accident business; how long it's been with me, whether it's still here. Certainly there are reminders. If I look out my window, I can see a group of city workmen in yellow hard-hats and luminescent vests. They're attacking a strip of pavement under which lies a ruptured water pipe. The men aren't particularly ambitious, but in the manner of experienced workers they effectively jack-hammer and shovel through pavement, gravel, clay – until they stand waist-deep in a trench. And for a moment, in memory, I stand there with them.

The part of France I knew in 1915 was a matrix of trenches, mud, lice, and unhappy men. I spent a long time there. There was nothing heroic in this. Like many others I was provided with a certain line of thought by a recruiting poster. I followed it, and came to a place where the sky sometimes exploded, and men and animals died; and little things, like dry socks, were important to me. And for a while I came to believe what the army – what everyone – seemed to have known all along: that order is good and confusion is bad. If I stayed in my trench, and climbed out of it only when I was told, I would probably survive. I trusted in this, because there was little else to trust in. I came to appreciate what most people in this civilization must see as simple fact: there's safety in conformity. Then one day a soldier named Mackleroy and I were cleaning our rifles, when we heard – above the muffled bumps of familiar artillery – a sound like a tea kettle boiling, far away. We only had time to look at each other. The sound boiled closer, and when it stopped there was an explosion. My trench, Mackleroy, and every thought I had about order disintegrated around me. I was wounded and buried in a sea of mud; and if I recall anything, it's not merely the pain, or the tedious hours I spent worming my way to fresh air, or my eventual rescue. No, what I remember is the force of this unpredictable thing that makes one man dead and another alive. I don't pretend to understand it, but I know it's there. Or I hope it's there. It's the accident business, and it makes one nurse old and another young, one man sighted and one woman blind.

A geyser of water shoots momentarily from the workmen's trench, and they scramble away cursing, water-splattered. Near the sidewalk another workman with his hand on the water valve laughs uproariously, and the spray subsides. This is the accident business, too.

SEPTEMBER 7: I make these journal entries in a green covered order book which once belonged to a company called Western Grocer's Supply. The paper has lines, and I do my best to write between them. That's the way I was taught; in fact, at the beginning of this century, a teacher named Carmichael used a ruler on my knuckles to impress upon me the importance of staying between the lines. Lines, it seems, are integral to this age we live in. There are air lines, enemy lines, unemployment lines, career lines, lines of work, lines of questioning. As a salesman for Western Grocer's, I followed a route line each week that led me across vast distances in this country, and back again. And if we want to get from here to there – from Carmichael's classroom and a lift-top desk to Sunset Home and Mrs Arnold's straight and narrow hallway – we've only to follow the lines. And watch where they intersect: to form wars, treaties, marriages, births – until at last they draw themselves out: to the end of the line.

And yet today, I considered staggering after Mrs Arnold to give her authoritative behind an authoritative goose, simply to see it swerve, or get off the ground.

There's no explaining the risks we run, the dangers we pursue.

SEPTEMBER 8: Emily waits for me near the dining room windows. She's tall and deep-bosomed, and poises her white cane in front of her, the way most blind people do. Her silhouette looks deceptively self-assured. I think of how stalwart she must've appeared to the decades of schoolchildren who filed into her classroom. Actually, she's nervous. 'What if it doesn't work?' she wonders. Her illness has left her paler than usual; the watery film that coats her eyes makes her look as though she's about to cry. But she stands erect. She has all the contradictory signs of someone at once fearful and cocky, foolish and wise. 'I'll talk to Schroeder,' I say. She smiled, and arm in arm we dodder into the dining room; I see for her, she walks for me. It occurs to me that we might look comic, lovable, old – except that to all our grey and grizzled friends here, our uncertain shuffle is commonplace. There are times, I tell Emily, when I wish I'd learned to tap-dance.

SEPTEMBER 10: At the centre of this building there's a walled-in garden, open to the sky. There are two cedar trees here, some rocks, and a number of benches. Schroeder and I sit in the sun, playing chess. Rather, Schroeder plays chess. He's trying to teach me, but I'm a hopeless pupil. His bald, freckled head is cocked to one side like a bird's; his bushy eyebrows knit together. Schroeder is the undisputed chess champion at the Home. Recently he's taken to playing himself, as he is now. Schroeder is trying to beat Schroeder, and it's his move.

He tells me about his son-in-law, who owns several small apartment buildings in a town some miles from this city. It's a modest town in the mountains, and has streets that meander over cliffs and into valleys and around rocky outcrops. There will be, Schroeder tells me, the pleasant, crisp smell of autumn and frost-nipped leaves. His son-in-law expects us by the end of the month. 'And you'll have to be there,' Schroeder says. 'My son-in-law can't hold a place that cheap forever.'

I ask Schroeder if he'd like to go with us. Not with his daughter living there, he says. Like many of us, Schroeder has a child who pays for the extravagance of this garden, these benches, those trees, the stipulation being that he can never leave. In the curious reversal peculiar to our times, our children have become our parents. We're the helpless now. It's a case of lines getting crossed, tangled, knotted. My own son pays a bundle to keep me here. He visits me once a year, at Christmas. There's no malevolence in this, I'm sure; it's just easier for him. It gives his year a uniformity, like the graphic read-out of a heartbeat on Mrs Arnold's electrocardiogram. Once a year – for my son, for Schroeder's daughter, for most of the other child benefactors of our wrinkled crew – the heart skips a beat, has a fibrillation, goes crazy for love. Once a year; then continues on, as regular as an ocean wave. Schroeder, in his attempts to get to his son-in-law, has had his shoes taken away and his overcoat hidden, on the orders of his sour and middle-aged daughter. Now he teaches me chess. He's content to show others all the moves.

'Watch this now.' With his pincher Schroeder moves a knight. Schroeder's pincher is made of aluminum alloy and works on cables connected to the muscles of his forearm. The hand was lost in France during the First War – the same war I was in. Neither Schroeder nor I have discovered why his hand lies in France, while both mine still hang on the ends of my arms. But by prehensile manipulation Schroeder shows me how a knight can attack, retreat, feint, or capture. I find this consoling. Schroeder's pincher may be capable of mere squeezes or claw-like grabs, but on the chessboard his knight appears to slash and twirl with the mobile fury of a matador.

In one daring move, Schroeder has captured his own queen.

SEPTEMBER 12:   In recent days, Emily and I have been walking around the grounds of the Home. Some of the leaves have fallen, withered and colourful, so that now they rustle around our feet like bits of scrap paper. 'City noises sound sharper in the fall,' Emily says. 'There's nothing to muffle them.' I stop, and lean expectantly into the blurred shapes of traffic and the whisper of tires. It's all noise to me.

We sit on a bench, near a small playground. Over by the swings, a harried young kindergarten teacher herds a mob of directionless kids towards a pedestrian cross-walk. One little boy stops to pee in the sand at the foot of the slide, to the delight of his classmates, the chagrin of his teacher. As a distraction, the teacher points out two crows trying to perch atop the same spruce tree. And for a moment, as I describe the scene to Emily, the glittering arch shot out by the boy looks as pure as glass, as innocent as a rainbow.

The children troop across the street to the bus stop; their reedy little voices argue over what they've seen that day, and how much of it they understand. At 3:15, by my watch, a bus slews lopsidedly around the corner and lurches to a stop, scattering the kindergarten class like a flock of chickens. The teacher herds them aboard, and the bus pulls away.

'That's the bus we'll take,' I tell Emily. She squeezes my hand. 'I haven't been on a bus in years,' she says.

SEPTEMBER 14:   Leaves, I notice, fall hysterically, and in no particular pattern.

SEPTEMBER 16:   There are arrangements that have to be

made. If there's to be travel, money, and survival in a small mountain town, then certain lines of action must be followed. I'm learning what a spider must know as innate truth, or reflex: that as we cast off the lines that bind, so must we manufacture new ones that will allow escape.

Today I went as far as the bank. The teller there thinks I'm cute. 'All that money, Mr Hurd?' she asks. 'In traveller's cheques,' I say. She's relieved at that. She's a kind person who wouldn't like to send an old codger loaded and unarmed out into a nasty world. So she won't be disillusioned, I tell her a lie about sons and grandchildren and their insistence on my sharing with them a trip to Hawaii. From past conversations I've come to recognize that for my bank teller there's always a Hawaii that shimmers like gold in some future sunset: a job promotion, a new car, or some other thing that measures how far along the line she's come. This is the promise of our age: that each of us will get his due. There have to be incentives for us to follow the long and sometimes inevitable track we find ourselves on. For Emily and me, Hawaii waits in a cheap basement suite in a small town in the mountains. But it isn't inevitable. And that's the difference.

So in spite of my lining up as others do, and receiving my wad and the teller's smile, I'm aware that there must be hope for the accident business. I might carefully plot a bus trip and reserve tickets over a pay phone to avoid Mrs Arnold's overhearing. I might talk to the assistant bank manager about the deposit and transfer of accounts and cheques. I might arrange all the other necessaries that will couple Emily's and my slender pensions to make possible food, heat, clothing, and some version of being free. I might do all these things. And I have.

Even so, the accident business waits: to attack or retreat, save or destroy.

SEPTEMBER 18: Maybe it's the unexpected that allows us to glimpse the pattern of things. This morning Mrs Arnold discovers me backing out of Emily's room. I'm wearing pajamas and carry my slippers in my hand, and these facts apparently remind Mrs Arnold of something religious. 'My God!' she hisses from behind me, and I turn to face her and the harsh hallway lights. I'm haggard and guilty, and if I say, 'Not God, only me,' it's to show Mrs Arnold that I, too, have a morality.

Mrs Arnold glares at me. I watch her. In the silence of the moment the opportunity for change hovers around us. We can – by altering the shape of our eyes, our mouths – change the shape of each other. A smile would start it, a laugh would make it final. I grin. I'm willing to let Mrs Arnold list me under a new column on her clipboard: as Emily's lover, as an old fool, as a mischievous fuddy-duddy. I prefer it, just as I'd prefer to consider Mrs Arnold as someone other than a fat, intimidating woman. But Mrs Arnold doesn't smile, or laugh. She points. 'Get back to the men's wing and your own room. *Now*. We will discuss this later.'

I go, attempting some dignity, though I feel her gaze on my retreating skinny ankles, which crackle like a piano player's knuckles. I hope she won't waken Emily and subject her to one of those rules-and-regulations harangues. Emily is a gentle person who at one time disciplined children. To be disciplined herself only recalls for her the injustice she might have inflicted on others, so many years ago.

I walk away sadly. It occurs to me that the rigidity of Mrs Arnold's hallway and the stiffness of arthritic joints have something in common: they lack humour.

The meeting with Mrs Arnold is accomplished behind a large rubber plant in the lounge. It is not merry. Mrs Arnold is interested in puritanism. She doesn't tell us this directly, but her murmured ethics imply it. 'You disappoint us,' she says. We huddle in the shadow of dark, shiny leaves, and the cool judgement of a professional. Simply put, Emily and I are to number ourselves among the ruins of our civilization. There are quaint relics which demand preservation, but which serve no useful purpose in this, the age of the progressive, the utilitarian, the feasible. Our sex organs – like butter churns or gramophones – must be allowed to wind down. 'At your age,' Mrs Arnold says.

She has mistaken comfort for passion, and if she sees at all the lines that lead backward from us to our beginnings in this century, she thinks of them as tied firmly, nostalgically, to stumps of romance, trees of youth. But we are to go no further.

'Reverend Peters will have to talk to you,' she says. Suspicion glitters in her eyes as she speaks to us. We are betrayers of some code invented by our own generation.

Oh, evil man.

Oh, fallen woman.

We will, Mrs Arnold's eyes suggest, bear watching.

SEPTEMBER 21:   Schroeder assures me that in the game of chess there is an infinite number of moves. The supper bell rings at precisely six o'clock. When she stands to observe me, Mrs Arnold folds her arms under bosom, parallel to the floor.

Time after time I'm forced to consider the pattern of our lives.

SEPTEMBER 24:   Reverend Peters, it seems, is a young man with a mission. At present he's trying to integrate most of the religions of the world into one flexible dogma. I wish him luck. While I try to unravel some of the lines and coils I've discovered or imagined, Peters is busy weaving more of them. His expressive hands tie knots out of thin air. He talks about reincarnation and Sioux Indians and karma. In the warp and woof of his eloquence he's lost Emily and me. Emily twines her fingers nervously. I sit in my chair and nod.

It occurs to me that one of the prices of growing old is to suffer the wisdom of the young.

And yet I admire Mr Peters. He's youthful, eager, and comfortable with his vision of hope. Apparently, we're much like the birds, flocking to some divine migratory route plan. Flyways have been mapped out for us. Serenity will be our nest.

Miss Shinkel appears and Reverend Peters stammers, then stops talking altogether. Emily smiles.

For all our sophistication, in the end we're suckers for love.

SEPTEMBER 27: Four days until we leave. I'm excited, and so is Emily: exhilarated, doubtful, giddy, scared. If anything, this move should reveal to us how much of the accident business is still ours to use. I consider the lines I've followed to arrive at this point: from soldier to husband to father to widower – to old man. Through processes unknown to me I've been led here – as Emily has, as Schroeder has, as Miss Shinkel has, as Reverend Peters has, as Tim Ecklestone *was*. Their lines are here, too. And as I write I see this: that unless we escape, or fall in love, or rage and whine at the end, we become lines ourselves. Our chins disappear into our necks, our notebooks become clipboard lists, and the world of clandestine love and peeing boys and workmen's fountains fades into the length of an empty hall.

In the garden, Schroeder slips Emily and me a vinyl travellers' chessboard. We are ready.

SEPTEMBER 30: As it pulls to a stop, the bus nudges my shoulder. Only slightly, but it's enough to sprawl me to my knees on the pavement, where I leave some skin and a few threads of trouser cloth. Emily and the driver pull me to my feet, and in the noise of an idling engine and their worried questions, I announce – maybe too loudly – that I'm all right.

I am all right.

Aboard and moving, I swivel stiffly to look back at the receding Sunset Home. Maybe it's Mrs Arnold I see, stark and white against the red bricks, standing on the steps. At this distance I can't be sure.

The motion of this bus makes it hard to write. My shoulder is sore.

The mountains, when we first sight them, are magnificent.

The Sample Case

WHEN THE TIME CAME for my grandfather's will to be read, my grandmother flung open the doors of her house and festively bustled from kitchen to dining room with pots of tea and trays of butter tarts. Sensible shoes and house dresses had always been her policy, but for this occasion she wore high-heeled pumps, pearls, and a salmon-coloured dress printed with whorled sea-shells.

'Your mother's bearing up well,' the lawyer told my father.

'She's a strong woman.' My father sipped his Scotch. 'You've got to give her that.'

The lawyer's name was Borowsky. He loosened his tie and over a glass of sherry told a story about my grandfather.

'I was a boy when I first saw Wilbur,' he said. 'He was under a horse on Seventh Street. This was when he first came to this country, when he drove the dray. The horse was a Percheron, a massive beast. Wilbur squatted under the horse's belly like a weight-lifter and another fellow went around the crowd collecting bets in his cap.' Borowsky sipped his sherry and watched us watching my long-ago grandfather. 'I'll never forget it. Wilbur didn't even grunt. Simply lifted; the horse rolled its eyes and snorted, then went still. Nobody made a sound. When all four hooves cleared the ground, the men applauded and the kids cheered. I remember I asked my dad who that was. "That's Wilbur Findlay," he said.'

Borowsky drained his glass. My grandmother fiddled with her pearl necklace. 'He was a fool,' she said.

'Now, Mother.' My father lifted his hand.

'You wouldn't know.' Grandmother smoothed her dress. 'That's how he ruined his back. Adolescent heroics.' As an immigrant from an industrial town in northern England, she could remember when the streets of her new city were mud. 'We needed the money in those days. Wilbur always fancied himself as a performer.'

Auntie Rose started to cry. Both she and Auntie Velma lived several hundred miles away and had flown in for the funeral. Though my grandfather's illness had been an extended one, and his death anticipated, Auntie Rose hadn't believed any of it until she viewed his body in the coffin. Now she sobbed openly. 'He always had so much energy,' she said.

'For Christ's sake, Rose,' Auntie Velma said. 'Don't start.' Of the three surviving children, Auntie Velma was considered the most cosmopolitan. She collected antiques, and wore dresses that showed her cleavage.

My father put his arm around Auntie Rose. 'There, there, Rosie,' he said.

'Don't patronize her, Gordon.' Auntie Velma lit a cigarette. 'And we can do without your usual observations on female hysteria.'

'I don't have any observations,' my father said.

My mother, who'd enlisted me to set chairs around the dining room table, intervened. 'I think we're ready to sit down now. David,' she told me, 'get a cushion for your gran.'

The table was oblong with gateleg leaves at either end so that we faced one another over the arc of an ellipse. I thought about my grandfather. During his illness I'd visited him daily, since the hospital was only a few blocks from my high school. I'd already heard from him how he'd lifted the horse. Near the end, his illness often carried him into the past. 'I've had a good life,' he said once, and humiliated, turned his head away to cry. 'Nancy never thought so, though.'

Nancy was my grandmother. Now, directly across from the lawyer, she folded her hands on the tabletop and waited.

Borowsky read the will in a calm, uninflected voice. Substantially everything was left to my grandmother, with the exception of some mementoes and personal belongings. The carpentry tools went to my father; the *Encyclopaedia Britannica* to Auntie

Rose. Auntie Velma received the rolltop desk on which he'd written his invoices every Friday night for thirty-seven years. The watercolours of Paris went to my mother.

I was left one hundred dollars and my grandfather's sample-case.

'There is, however, a condition attached to this last item.' Borowsky looked at my grandmother. 'It involves you, Mrs Findlay.'

'What condition?'

'That you and your grandson drive Wilbur's former sales route and distribute the contents of the sample-case.'

'Contents?' my grandmother said. 'What contents?'

'I'm not privy to that information,' Borowsky said. 'The sample-case is to be opened by your grandson David the day of your departure. The trip,' he consulted the will, 'is to be completed within seven days of the reading of this document.'

My grandmother shifted in her chair. 'Is this legal?'

'Absolutely.'

Auntie Velma drew on her cigarette and blew smoke towards the ceiling.

My father chuckled.

'I don't see what's so funny, Gordon,' my grandmother said. 'Your father must've drawn this up when he was full of those drugs they were giving him.'

Borowsky shook his head. 'Wilbur came to me well over a year ago, Mrs Findlay.'

'Capriciousness.' My grandmother looked to her children for confirmation. 'A whim.'

'It's what he wanted, Mum.' Auntie Rose smiled radiantly, transfigured by this evidence from beyond the grave of my grandfather's sense of justice.

My grandmother jutted her recalcitrant chin at the lawyer. 'Are you sure I'm legally bound by this nonsense?'

Borowsky shrugged. 'The will could be contested.'

My grandmother studied all of the faces around the table and settled on my father's. He was a carpenter, and in a way peculiar to his profession had a face of straight-grained openness and integrity.

'You would, wouldn't you, Gordon?'

'It's his will, Mother.'

The others nodded. Auntie Velma said it would only take a few days to make the trip. 'A few perfunctory farewells. You know how sentimental he was.'

My grandmother finally capitulated, but with wounded dignity, like a reputable general signing a surrender in the presence of enemies she knew to be inferior. Quietly seething, she fixed us with pale blue eyes and issued commands. The car would have to be checked over. Reservations at hotels would have to be made. An itinerary of the trip would have to be plotted.

'And I'll want to see the sample-case,' she said.

'I'm to give it to David.' Borowsky rubbed his nose.

'He's just a boy. Still in school.'

'Nonetheless, I'm to give it to him.'

She signed the documents. We all did. Mrs Baker from next door was called in as a witness. Then Borowsky packed his brief-case, thanked us, and left. Through the veranda windows we watched him step down the front walk, skirting the fingers of yellow leaves that reached across the pavement. His sleek car glided away under the leafless boulevard trees.

'I believe that man was laughing,' my grandmother said.

Later when I got home I locked myself in my room and opened the sample-case – a sharp-edged black leather case with a thick wooden handle worn smooth by all those years of being slung in and out of the back seats of cars. The case contained twenty-seven sealed white envelopes, each numbered, and each addressed to a person I didn't know. There were only the envelopes in the case; otherwise it was empty.

THE NIGHT BEFORE we were to leave I dreamed about my grandfather. I tried to glimpse him as he was before his illness – at his lakeside cottage in his swimsuit, tanned, squat as a sumo wrestler, bellowing as he plunged into the water. But in my dream, his flesh dissolved, his colour paled, his thatch of hair thinned. he became his hospital self, as thin and brittle as kindling. Scrawny, spindle-legged, he stumbled into the green water and disappeared. He washed up later on the sand, a bundle of sticks to be stored in the cottage shed among the kayak paddles and croquet mallets.

I woke up in the grey light with the house creaking around me. On the bedside table the road map lay open: eleven hundred miles of narrow highways and gravel roads, which had led my grandfather to all those small towns for thirty-seven years. Some of those places names I could reel off by heart – Shell River, White Fox, Star City, Spence's Corner, St. Brieux, Ermine Lake, Lantern Lake, Parksdale, Carlyle, Arbourvale – a litany of cafés and general stores, grain elevators and gas stations. He'd memorized them all, wheeled his car along the length of their Main Streets, watched them recede in his rear-view mirror so he could make it home every Friday night.

I pitied him. I wanted to tell him his mistake, his miscalculation. Those eleven hundred miles hadn't led him anywhere.

THE TRIP took five days. North of the city the rolling farmland ambitiously heaved itself into substantial hills. Bluffs of poplar gave way to forests of evergreens. At first each town seemed exceptional in some way; one had a view of a lake, another a domed Greek Orthodox church, another a gleaming water tower with the town's name emblazoned on the side. Despite her apparent indifference my grandmother sat brightly in the front seat and watched the countryside stream by. Some of the autumn leaves hadn't fallen, and she exclaimed at these unexpected flames of colour.

But inevitable monotony took over; as the sky grew overcast the trees and fields blurred indistinctly, like smudged paint. Topping a rise, the highway sliced through the trees ahead of us, an arrow pointed at infinity. Each town had its café, its gas station, its grain elevator, its hotel. The same men in the same baseball caps climbed out of the same muddy pickup trucks and straggled into the same beer parlours. In stump-ridden pastures white-faced cattle stood with their tails to the wind and stared morosely into the oncoming winter.

'Bush,' my grandmother commented. 'At one time Wilbur wanted to buy a farm out here.'

'Why didn't he?'

'I talked some sense into him.' She looked at the window. 'Just look at it.'

In the beginning she handed over the envelopes shyly, looking away when the man or woman behind the counter exclaimed in wonder, or held my grandfather's message at arm's length for her to verify.

'He wishes me luck,' one woman said. 'He says I'll get a refund on that detergent he had in the display.'

In another town a store manager pulled a dollar out of the envelope. 'I'm supposed to have a beer on him.'

'He never drank alcohol while he was working,' my grandmother said.

'Beer?' the man said. 'Beer isn't alcohol.'

In Shell River the store owner gave us a photograph of my grandfather taken in 1934. He wore his hat pushed back on his head and rested his right foot on the running board of his car. His suit looked new.

'I remember when he bought that suit,' my grandmother said. 'We couldn't really afford it.'

Later in the car she leaned her head back into the seat and closed her eyes. 'He used to come home exhausted,' she said. 'No doubt the banality wore him out.'

I drove as I thought my grandfather would have: fast and relentless, watching the car hood swallow the miles.

The first night we stayed at a small motel so near the highway that all-night logging trucks rattled the windows as they passed. At two o'clock in the morning my grandmother came to my room and told me to get some earplugs from the night clerk. I pulled my clothes over my pajamas and walked outside to the office.

The night was clear and still; only the stars saw me. The manager didn't have earplugs, but he scrounged some cotton batting from his first aid kit. I gave this to my grandmother.

'I know what you're thinking,' she said, 'You're thinking what a bitch she is.'

I'd never heard my grandmother swear before. 'I'm not thinking that.'

'Of course you are,' she said. She had her coat on over her nightgown. Blue Orlon slippers poked out from under the hem like a couple of fuzzy stuffed animals. 'And you're right. I am a bitch. I always was. But that's what Wilbur needed. Somebody to keep house and home together, somebody to tell him how to budget his pay. Oh, I know,' she sat down on my bed, and I grew alarmed. 'I know,' she continued. 'Everybody loved Wilbur, he was a big-hearted man. And he worked hard. Driving all those miles – the roads weren't paved in the early days, you know.' She scowled at me accusingly, as if I thought the early days were a piece of cake. 'But we both worked hard. I didn't have electricity until 1935. Or running water until the war. And five kids to look after –' She watched my face. 'Ah,' she said. 'You didn't know, did you? Yes, we had five, Wilbur and me. Two other boys, John and Albert. John died of whooping cough when he was two. Bertie – Albert – was ten months old. He went colicky and just died – in his sleep.'

'I didn't know that, Gran. I'm sorry.'

'Oh,' she said. 'Don't be. It was years ago.' But her head was down. She stood barely over five feet, and sitting on my bed she looked smaller. Her feet dangled off the floor. 'It was a relief in some ways. They wore me out, those kids. When I knew I was pregnant again, I flung myself down the basement stairs to get rid of it. I never told Wilbur, of course.'

'What happened?'

'Nothing,' she said. 'That was your Auntie Rose.'

The next morning I had to scrape frost off the windshield. The wind smelled of winter, a crisp chill around the nostrils. We drove for an hour and a half and arrived at a village called

Spence's Corner. In the general store a fat man in a stained white shirt took the envelope from my grandmother and tore it open with his thumb. When he grinned his false teeth did something spectacular to his face. 'You gotta match me for a cigar, Mrs Findlay.'

'I beg your pardon?'

'You gotta match me for a cigar. Wilbur did, every time he came through.'

The man's name was Scotty. He fished a quarter out of the cash register. He flipped the coin in the air and slapped it plumply on the back of his hand. 'Call it.'

'Is that what he says in the letter?'

'Sure. Call it.'

'Tails.'

Scotty uncovered the coin. 'I owe you a cigar.'

'I don't smoke.'

But Scotty dug under the counter and came up with a fat Havana. 'Don't look a gift horse in the mouth, Mrs Findlay. That's my motto.' He handed her the cigar. 'There's a Cuban someplace who worked a couple of hours for a banana to roll this beauty. We don't want to waste it.'

Scotty had known my grandfather for over twenty years. As we went out the door he called, 'They got a kid on his route now, Mrs Findlay. He's doing okay, but he ain't Wilbur.'

My grandmother put the cigar in her purse. 'Accolades,' she said. 'Wouldn't Wilbur be proud.'

The weather turned ominous. Skiffs of snow blew across the road like wavering sheets of hard white sand. I strained to see the centre line on the pavement. The earth disappeared; we drove on a cloud, touching down long enough to keep us from the ditch. The car felt lighter. When I looked in the rear-view mirror, an opaque plume of snow roiled behind us. On the back seat the sample case lay as motionless as a coffin.

In the next town a woman opened the envelope and gave my grandmother a chocolate cake. In St. Brieux an old man with gnarled hands offered to give my grandmother a back rub. 'I

used to be a masseur,' he said. 'I gave Jimmy McClarnen a rub-
down after he lost the title.'

And so it went. At each shop my grandmother handed the
store owner an envelope and suffered in silence as he promised
her a pineapple or a sonata on a violin or a rousing good game of
cribbage. At the Value-Save in Parksdale the butcher's wife
asked for ten dollars. 'We're building a new Legion Hall,' she
explained. 'Wilbur always gave.' We spent the second night at
the Gold Plate Hotel in Carlyle, the third at the Kapasawin
Motor Lodge which overlooked the deserted beach and grim
grey waters of Lantern Lake. Between driving and cups of coffee
and standing on cracked linoleum or oiled floors or spanking
new tiles under fluorescent lights, my grandfather's work life
unrolled in stages, like a carpet down a flight of stairs. One man
snatched the envelope from my grandmother's fingers and tore it
in half without looking at it. 'I'm sorry,' he said. 'But nothing that
son of a bitch has written would interest me.' Another simply
refused the envelope, claiming it was addressed to the previous
owner, who he thought had moved to Arizona.

We ate in truck-stop cafes, surrounded by pot-bellied drivers
in felt-pack boots that smelled of diesel fuel and coffee. The
wind dropped, and the first real snow of the year fell in thick,
heavy flakes. Snow ploughs flashed their blue lights like beacons
on the highway, their engines muffled in the still air. As we
drove, the stillness entered the car; my grandmother sat pen-
sively, her hands folded in her lap. She squinted into the billow-
ing snow and I wondered if she were trying to see into the future,
having come this far from the past. What had my grandfather
expected of her on this trip – rounded as it was in the soft curves
of freshly fallen snow, visible only when the sign for the next
town loomed from the edge of the highway? What were we supposed to sample, carrying that case from one stop to the next?
The pile of envelopes had dwindled; we were ahead of schedule.
Weather permitting, we would be home in four days instead of
five.

At the next junction I turned off the highway onto a narrow

unploughed road. The green sign told us where we were headed: Arbourvale.

My grandmother looked at her watch. 'It's only one o'clock,' she said. 'We're doing well.'

THE STORE OWNER'S NAME was Berenson. He was middle-aged; an open face, short cropped grey hair, a wide neck that sloped to narrow heavily-muscled shoulders. He had that same thickness about him, and a way of cocking his small round head so that at certain moments the resemblance was uncanny. But if my grandmother noticed it she remained composed: she introduced herself and handed him the envelope. He opened it unhurriedly, glancing up now and then in sceptical amusement, as if we were curious but harmless creatures whose fears he was at pains to allay.

'Please sit down,' he said. He'd carried two chairs from his cubbyhole office, one in each hand.

But my grandmother preferred to stand. She knew him by then. Of all my grandfather's children this Berenson was most like him. Thick-chested, short-limbed, he could've squatted under a Percheron and lifted it to cheers and admiring applause, grinning his Findlay grin. If resurrection was truth, then it was truth I saw there, behind the counter of Berenson's Red and White Store; Wilbur Findlay stood pretty much as I remembered him before his illness – hale, hearty and ready to laugh.

Berenson read his letter slowly. 'He wants you to come in and have a cup of tea,' he said. 'I'll just tell my mother. Please sit down, Mrs Findlay.'

My grandmother sat down. Berenson moved through the aisles to a door at the back of the store. He even walked like my grandfather, shoulders rolling.

My grandmother shifted her purse on her lap and averted her face. 'If you say one word, David,' she said, 'I will get up and slap you.'

We sat without speaking until Berenson called us.

The narrow kitchen smelled of cooking oil and new paint. We

left our overshoes at the door. The woman who met us was large, and what'd once been pretty in her face had, through weariness and humour, softened into comfortable folds. She stood to one side of the kitchen table, an awkward hostess.

'Come in, Mrs Findlay. Please sit down. I'm Miriam Berenson,' she added, as if it explained something.

'How do you do,' my grandmother said. 'This is my grandson David.'

Mrs Berenson studied me; her eyes were green, flecked with light and I saw what my grandfather must've seen. 'Hello,' she said. She addressed her son. 'Frank, perhaps you'd like to show David the shop for a few minutes. I'll call you when the tea's made.'

Frank led me through the cramped living room to a workshop that'd been added to the back of the building. Corkscrews of wood shavings littered the floor. There was a table saw and a bench of tools, a lathe, and several bins of sweet-smelling wood.

'I putter around in here,' Frank Berenson said. 'I make furniture. Coffee tables, bookshelves, cabinets, that sort of thing.' He picked up a spindle that'd just been turned on the lathe. 'Your dad's a carpenter, isn't he?'

'Yes.'

'Wilbur used to say I should move. Said there'd be a market for this kind of thing in a bigger place.'

It was the only time that afternoon that Frank Berenson mentioned his father.

In the kitchen we drank tea and ate date squares and puffed wheat cake. My grandmother and Mrs Berenson had settled into small talk about the weather and the condition of the roads. What'd passed between them I could only guess; perhaps, like Frank Berenson and I, they found no need to put their shared absurdity into words. When it was time to go they stood and shook hands with polite amiability, as if tolerance could almost be reached and fools almost forgiven.

Yet as I swung the empty sample-case into the back seat of the car, and turned to wave to Frank Berenson, I felt bereft of something. Not of my grandfather, exactly. But something – as if, like travelling salesmen, we'd given away a free sample with no hope of a sale.

The snow stopped. White and unmarked, the world lay steeped in silence and its own luminous glare. I rolled down the driver's side window to clear the fogged windshield. The cold air stung the side of my face. When we reached the highway I rolled the window back up. The pavement had been ploughed, though dotted with slabs of packed snow where the grader's blade had ridden too high. I drove cautiously, suspecting ice.

'She called him Willie,' my grandmother said, and started to cry.

I saw her head dip as she fumbled with the latch of her purse. 'Gran, do you want me to stop?'

'Of course not.' Her purse was open. Her hand fell on something – the cigar she'd won. She rolled down the window and flung it into the roaring wind.

She dabbed her eyes with a kleenex. After a while she said, 'How many envelopes do we have left?'

'None. That was the last.'

She crossed her feet, uncrossed them again. 'I expect we were both fools.'

I had no answer to that. I turned on the headlights, though it wasn't dusk yet. The sky darkened but only at the perimeter of an infinite arc; beneath the sky, we drove through a dome of the snow's own peculiar light.

'It wasn't fair of him, Gran.'

She reached over and patted my arm. 'No, David, it wasn't.'

Several miles later she said, 'I suppose I should've left them my address.'

'They probably have it.'

'Yes, they probably do. And anyway, they're in the phone book, aren't they?'

'I think so.'

We drove in silence after that. The dome of light dropped lower, grey clouds scudded along the horizon. It was dark when we reached the city. Streetlights lit up the boughs of trees filigreed with garlands of snow. The drifts in front of my grandmother's house glittered with a million jewelled lights, so delicate that when I stopped the car we didn't get out right away, but sat wonderingly, as if seeing the place for the first time.

Thirty-three Thousand Push-ups

AFTER HIS MARRIAGE foundered and his wife took his children to live with his brother with whom she may or may not have been sleeping, Sadler shut up his suburban house and rented a furnished suite above a downtown gymnasium called Cormy's. Formerly a music store, Cormy's Gym catered to tattooed power lifters, spar-hardened boxers, and short-haired women. Now and then a few flatulent old men were allowed to lounge on a bench along one wall because they regaled the gym regulars with tales of strongmen from a bygone era, and because in that part of the city flatulent old men had nowhere else to go. There was a fine sense of dereliction surrounding Cormy's and Sadler, intent on moping, hated to see it go to waste.

What he hadn't counted on, however, was the intense activity of the place. Open sixteen hours a day, subject to the creak and clank of barbells and wall pulleys, grunts of lifters, thumps of heavy bags, and on Wednesdays the communal bellowing of a senior citizens' karate class, the gym was as noisy as a steel mill.

At first the racket got on Sadler's nerves; it rattled through the floor boards and threatened his crockery and bookshelves. He thought of complaining to Cormy, but the gym-owner had no neck and in the past Sadler had found such people recalcitrant. So he held his peace; gradually the din lulled him into familiarity, so that a month after he moved in he bought himself a gym membership.

It was an extravagance he could little afford. As a matter of pride he'd resigned his position as warehouse manager of his brother's printing firm. Living on his severance pay until he could find other work, he'd moved out of his house mainly because at night he fancied he could hear his children's voices in the empty rooms, because the red brick patio he stepped across each morning had been laid with much sweat and co-operation by him and his wife, and because the position of the furniture,

the angle of the door frames and the nap of the carpet all pro-
claimed his wife's tread, her smile, the shape of her head. On the
financial side, Sadler calculated he could meet the mortgage
payments for another three months, but once winter came and
the heating bills rolled in, he'd have to say good-bye to his home
forever. For this reason he'd listed the house for sale with a fiery
real estate agent named Larry Francis. Sadler hoped that once
the place was sold, peace would descend on him like a cloud or a
warm wool blanket, and the nightmares that had plagued him
since his separation would go away.

The dreams weren't so much terrifying as enervating. In his
sleep, his house took on the threat of some monstrous weight.
The colossal images of old-time strongmen painted by the old
men who hung around Cormy's invaded Sadler's dreams: he
often saw himself in a leopard-skin leotard and sandals, hauling
his house with his teeth as if it were a rail car loaded with pig-
iron. He bent stainless steel mortgages with his bare hands,
crumpled bank rates into iron filings, and once shouldered his
wife, kids, *and* his brother and pressed them overhead in a mon-
umental if clumsy one-armed lift. The credibility of these
dreams tired him – Sadler was a lean, fine-boned man more
suited to distance-running than to weight-lifting – and he sometimes woke from them dry-mouthed and exhausted.

Even so, he liked the atmosphere at Cormy's. There was none
of the narcissism so rampant in the more upscale health clubs.
(Cormy's had no carpets, no Muzak, and the only mirror was
used by the boxers), and in these austere surroundings he had
little chance of bumping into former business acquaintances who
might embarrass him with pity or lame excuses about why they
couldn't hire him. Sadler had phoned several businesses when
Verna made her tearful preference clear; most of them said the
same thing – that they had nothing at the moment, but would
keep him in mind. What they meant was that he was too old
(forty-three) to look for miracles. As well, he recognized that his
life had changed irrevocably and that he had no idea what to do

about it. For the moment, working out at Cormy's gave him focus.

He lifted weights and ran, and was very big on calisthenics because they involved much repetition and the lugubrious sense that he was accomplishing something. Sit-ups, for instance, he performed so frequently that he wore out two pairs of gym shorts in under six weeks. Push-ups – that punishment he recalled from a brief stint as a high-school football player – he performed with tedious satisfaction. Penitence, penitence, he murmured as he raised and lowered his body from the floor. He'd failed Verna and the kids somehow. (Verna: There were times during his push-ups that his body position and movement – up and down, up and down – ambushed him with erotic reveries. In some way Sadler didn't like to speculate about, his atonement for whatever sins he'd committed possessed an element of pleasure.)

'A lot of people would call that sick,' Mr Sundbo, the oldest, least flatulent observer on the bench pointed out. 'They'd throw Freud and Jung in there and mess up your mind. The fact is push-ups resemble screwing, that's all. Don't worry about it.'

'I'm not worried about it.'

The old man ignored his answer. Mr Sundbo had been a long distance walker in his youth; had tramped from Montreal to New Orleans on three pairs of shoes in 1931 and was used to going on. 'People thought *I* was crazy. But I wasn't crazy. I just wasn't very *bright*.'

When he wasn't in the gym, Sadler was out looking for a job. But in government manpower offices, in employment agencies, in waiting rooms, he was faced with lines of others like himself; those who through bad luck or bad timing found their talent and experience unwanted, until they began to doubt they *had* talent or experience. The only jobs he landed were part-time: taking stock, unloading trucks, and writing copy for a furniture sale flyer.

'Then why don't you ask Uncle Lloyd to give you your old job back?' Sadler's fifteen-year-old son asked him on a visit. 'He *would*, you know. He's sorry about what happened. So is Mum.'

'I'll find something.' Sadler stoutly echoed the words of his father, an ill-educated Second World War veteran who'd spent his life stooped over one manual-labouring job after another until cancer of the prostate finally released him to a holiday in eternity. Sadler's mother had remarried and gone to live on Vancouver Island among goats and pottery, so it seemed to him he was starting life over, without parents, wife, or – according to Justin – children.

'Me and Tammy are okay.' Justin had done something to his hair. It looked like a garden rake on fire.

'Tammy and *I*. Look, what's with the hair?'

'Oh, great. Mum said you'd say something about my hair. Something repressive.'

'Repressive? Who's repressive?'

'Oppressive, then.'

'*Op*pressive? *Re*pressive? What do you guys do now, play Scrabble?'

'We talk, that's all. We don't yell. Lloy- Uncle Lloyd doesn't see the point in yelling. He says we're rational beings.'

'Rational? When we were kids Lloyd tied me to a tree and threw darts at my head.'

'Dad – you and Uncle Lloyd are different, that's all.'

'Oh, I don't know. We have the same taste in women.' .

Justin looked shyly away. They sat on Sadler's bed, from where they could have catalogued most of the apartment's contents. 'You know, Dad, Mum says if you look at this positively, you'd see you were free.'

'Right. No encumbrances.'

'What she means is you don't have to worry about us. We miss you and everything, but you're not tied to us any more. You can do anything you want.'

'I can fly, I can fly.'

'Come on, Dad.'

When they said good-bye, Sadler hugged Justin longer than he'd planned, and with more fervour than the boy was used to.

Parting, they both agreed that if nothing else, Cormy's Gym had certainly added vitality to Sadler's embrace.

STRENGTH, THEN, became central to his life, and under the tutelage of the gym's instructor, Grissom (himself a former body-builder), Sadler's physique underwent a metamorphosis usually touted by mail-order strongmen on the back covers of certain men's magazines. And their claims were true: Sadler's waistline shrank, his shoulders broadened, his chest deepened and his arms, though not massive, looked as stringy as a blacksmith's. In fact, all the clichés of health and well-being presented themselves in Sadler's new body. He even stopped smoking. And since his life was reborn, or at least reconstructed, who was to say this physical renaissance wasn't profound? He felt youthful, springy, resurrected. The gym regulars complimented his appearance and stamina, and Mr Sundbo kept tabs on his accomplishments. 'Two hundred on the bench press, fella. Three hundred on the squats. One thousand forty-three push-ups in one hour.' The attention revived Sadler's optimism, and at times when his own workout was done he surveyed others' exertions with a tolerant and empathetic camaraderie.

One lifter in particular, a short slight woman with close-cropped hair, held his interest. Her name was Jane Sheard and she was trying for a world squat record. She rarely spoke to any-one except Grissom. Though she was muscular, her face was as lean as an aesthete's, and her movements expressed a meditative concentration. She worked quietly through her lifts, merely grunting when she shouldered poundages that would have buckled Sadler in half. She lifted with a grace and fluidity that he found astonishing. He admired Jane Sheard.

There was nothing sexual in this, though she was well-formed and swelled provocatively in her gym shorts. What Sadler noticed more than her body was her face. No matter what the lift, no matter how overwhelming the stress, her face remained com-posed. Stupidity might have accounted for her serenity, but Sadler guessed not. He once heard her tell Grissom that weight-lifters were active post-Darwinists. 'We evolve by shouldering our own dissatisfactions,' she said. Her quarrel, if she had one, was with a universe that had made her small and slight and female. She defied the stars, Sadler reasoned – for wasn't lifting six hundred pounds a mockery beyond mere gravity? Wasn't it really a barefaced challenge not simply against a weight, but against common sense, logic, reason itself? If a person like Jane Sheard (she weighed only one hundred and eighteen pounds) could face such odds with equanimity, wasn't there hope for the rest of us? Can't I, thought Sadler, do the same?

HE ARRANGED to meet his wife at a restaurant where he asked her if what she had in mind was divorce.

'I don't know yet, Charlie.'

'Are you sleeping with Lloyd?'

'What kind of question is that?'

Sadler shrugged. He didn't know what kind of question it was, but he had others. One of his shortcomings as a husband and father had been that when he was angry or upset he asked a lot of questions, for which he then supplied the answers. Rhetorical negativity, Verna called it. Sadler could remember when once, after eight years of marriage, Verna decided she wanted to move back to Saskatchewan to study veterinary medicine. She'd been a farm girl when he met her, and he suspected a nostalgia for milk cows and ducks. He'd turned his rhetorical negativity loose, then: 'How will we pay your tuition? Where will I find a job? What about the kids, they're still in diapers, for God's sake! How will we ever afford such a move? Jesus, Verna, the course lasts seven *years*!'

And so on. Even now, when he should have known better with his wife seated across from him surrounded by strangers, her familiar beauty unfamiliar now, questions boiled up in him:

'Are you going to marry Lloyd?'

'I'm not sure.'

'Because if you do you'll be legally bound to the same name. You'll still be Mrs Sadler, unless of course you want to revert to your maiden name. I think Justin and Tammy should have a choice of names, though, don't you? Maybe they could hyphenate their surname – Sadler-Sadler. What do you think?'

'Stop it, Charlie.'

'Or maybe they could invent new names. Justin could call himself Justin Hair. Tammy might like Tammy O. Pressed.'

'Charlie, please.'

'Okay. I'm sorry.' Sadler stopped long enough to toy with his napkin. Where they were paper, Sadler could be a napkin shredder. 'Listen, Verna, I had a dream the other night. I've been dreaming a lot lately. I dreamed you and the kids were trapped in a temple – like the temple we saw in Greece that time – remember? Before we had the kids? You were trapped in there and the columns were shuddering – it must've been an earthquake or something – and the temple started to collapse. It fell apart the way they do in those biblical epics Hollywood used to make. Remember? Victor Mature pushing over the columns, or was he trying to hold them up? Anyway, Victor wasn't there, Verna – only me. Don't you get it? I think I was pushing the temple over. Jesus, Verna, what are we doing? Why are we meeting in a restaurant? Aren't we supposed to be holding up temples or something?'

'Oh, Charlie.' Verna cradled her coffee cup between her hands. 'Do you think it's that easy?'

'It could be that easy.' Sadler almost believed himself. 'Why can't it be that easy?'

'I have slept with Lloyd.'

'Ah. Well.'

He wanted to hold her. He wanted to invite her back into the temple. *Help me pick up these bricks, Verna. We built a patio once, remember?* He wanted to tell her there were people who could squat six hundred pounds. *People change,* he wanted to say. *I can do more push-ups than you ever thought possible, Verna. I'm a new man.* But such simple-minded confessions might lead him to shaky ground – more earthquakes, he realized; so instead he told her about Cormy's Gym.

He described his workout and Jane Sheard and old Mr Sundbo. As he talked it seemed to him he was improvising a new and legitimate philosophy based on the metaphysics of fitness – as if the soul too had muscles, as if all human spirit needed was a brisk workout, as if love, loyalty and compassion could be won through discipline, repetition, and sweat. 'We evolve by shouldering our own dissatisfactions,' he heard himself saying. 'We accept them and go on from there.'

'Charlie,' Verna smiled sadly. 'You sound like one of those guests they have on talk shows, one of those people who've invented a car that runs on cucumbers.'

'Maybe I have, Verna. Maybe I've changed.'

'But in what way?'

'I don't know. You're welcome to find out. Larry Francis tells me he has a buyer for the house. He'll know for sure by Friday.' Sadler took a breath, felt his ribs try to expand. 'Somebody else is going to get our patio, Verna.'

He reached forward to take one of her hands, and she allowed him, for a moment. Her fingers were strong, finely shaped, and he thought he might think of them caressing his brother, but he didn't. Instead he saw her hand stroking the brows of his children when they were sick, saw her pull weeds from rose beds, fold laundry, scoop leftover rice from a pot. That a hand as familiar as his own should now appear extraordinary filled him with wonder and hope.

'Let's go home, Verna. Let's go back.'

But weeping, she said she couldn't go back. 'You say we evolve by shouldering our dissatisfactions, Charlie? What about me? I shouldered my dissatisfactions. Have I evolved? What did I evolve into? You're lonely and I'm sorry for that. But don't mistake loneliness for love, Charlie. I know what that's like. Don't mistake loneliness for love.' And she withdrew her hand and left.

At his table Sadler sat alone for so long that in the end one of the waiters had to ask him to leave.

HOW THEN do you explain a forty-three-year-old man down in

front of his brother's house doing push-ups? What penance or triumph does he seek when in gym shorts and running shoes – and gloves to protect his hands from sidewalk grit – he raises and lowers himself in the monotony of exercise? What is he trying to prove?

'The record for the most push-ups in a twenty-four-hour period is 32,573,' announces Mr Sundbo, whose voice rings rather loudly on this otherwise quiet, tree-lined, residential street. The small crowd that has gathered murmurs; a few people laugh, not in derision, exactly, but in amazement that such an activity with its dubious standard and purpose should have invaded their neighbourhood. The crowd is a mixture of the curious and sceptical: kids, mainly – teenagers in bright summer T-shirts, little gaffers on tricycles; a few stay-at-home mothers or fathers who stand with their hands in their pockets or arms folded across their middles; bemused commuters, male and female, still hot and sticky from the city, still clutching their briefcases, arrested between curb and front door by Sadler's vigour at a time of the day when the sun has dropped below the level of the trees and a cold drink is required before the barbecue can be lit.

As the evening wears on most of the crowd will drift away and return; periodically they will carry their drinks to their living-room windows or front steps to ascertain Sadler's progress. In time they will see that Mr Sundbo has gone, replaced by Sadler's son who sits in a lawn chair, a pad, pencil and calculator balanced on his knees; still later they will notice Sadler's daughter sitting there too, a jug of lemonade at her feet, an alarm clock in her hand. And in front of them Sadler performs his push-ups – up, down, up, down – through sunset and twilight and on into the darkness when the streetlights cast leafy shadows over the pavement, and bats, uttering high shrill cries, ride the night air.

By morning, of course, Sadler will be gone. World records, however preposterous, are elusive. The neighbours will rise and discover in his absence a vague feeling of disappointment and betrayal, while at the same time they will smugly allow that his achievement was pointless anyway, if not juvenile. And forgetting, they will fall into the routine of their lives. It is only later, in conversation with each other and with the brother who now lives alone, that they will learn that Sadler and his wife and family left together, and that together they have moved away.

Flying

IT WAS A TWEED OVERCOAT, heavy as thick burlap. Grissom kept a healthy wad of it fisted tightly in his right hand.

'You're not going anywhere, bub,' Grissom told the thin man. 'You can just forget it.'

The thin man stopped squirming and went limp again, suspended loosely in his overcoat like a puppet. The cold wind lifted wisps of the thin man's hair. He waggled his bony head and stared down at the water.

'Flappity-flap,' he said.

'Not a chance,' Grissom said. 'I told you already.'

The thin man slumped. On the riverbank below them a small crowd gathered. A few people oooed when they saw the thin man move. The spar of the railway trestle dug into Grissom's thick chest. The thin man dangled from his hand like a skinny baby in a jolly jumper.

Grissom's hand fell asleep. Tiny needles prickled the ends of his fingers, blood ran away up his arm. Between distant silhouette houses the flashing red light of a police car winked among the sidestreets and the evening traffic. Somewhere the train, already past this trestle and the next one and out on the fringes of the city, blared to the suburbs and the patches of countryside. Grissom considered the police car.

'Just a few more minutes,' he said.

The thin man cheered up. He twisted his head around and for a moment the whites of his eyes glittered in the fading light. 'They'll never make it,' he said. His breath smelled of tooth powder.

Below, the river flowed like cold ink, lighter where patches of oil swirled iridescent patterns on its surface. Bobbing flecks of white dotted the water: Grissom wondered if they were gulls or garbage. From under the bridge a pigeon rode a crest of wind, wheeled sharply, and with a breaking flutter perched clumsily on one of the iron beams near the two men. The pigeon puffed his feathers and cooed in the cold. Grissom watched the bird.

'Hey, bub, you know about those things. Do they have air in their feathers or what?'

The streetlights went on, a blink of fluorescent blue. The streets were narrow tunnels of secret light. The thin man watched them.

'Do they have air in their feathers?' Grissom said.

The thin man glanced at the bird. 'Feathers stand on end, like hairs. The barbules trap air in the spaces and the bird warms it with his body heat.' The thin man smiled, a line drawn in custard. 'Read Audubon's book when this is over.'

'I'll borrow your copy.'

'Hee, hee.'

'You'll still be around.'

'Optimism is so pathetic,' the thin man said. 'A man your age.'

Grissom's fingers grew numb. He would have to change hands. The thin man hadn't been heavy at first, how could he have been? On his initial leap the tweed overcoat ballooned out and snagged the protruding bridge spar. The coat hadn't ripped. The cloth held, even as the thin man bucked and writhed to free himself from its folds. The cloth held, allowing Grissom time to clamber up the slope and along the bridge and down to the thin man's perch. Now the thin man was a sack of bricks and horseshoes. Grissom's sweatsuit stuck to his back. His legs were braced under another spar. He relieved the pressure from the backs of his legs by alternately bending his knees.

'The thing about birds,' the thin man was saying, 'is they can fly whenever they want to. Whenever they want to. Caw, caw.' He moved his arms. 'That's the thing about birds.'

'Right.' Grissom said. 'That's birds in a nutshell. They got wings, and they fly. It's one of life's goddamn miracles.'

'There's no need to be nasty.'

'Nasty. Oh boy. Nasty? You wouldn't know nasty if it crawled up your nose. You'd think this was my idea.'

'It is,' the thin man said.

'Oh boy.' Grissom shifted his weight. 'I feel really lucky I met you. I feel very fortunate, you know what I mean?'

'His brother's keeper,' the thin man said.

'How's that?'

'You're your brother's keeper.' The thin man nearly smiled.

'I am not.'

'Certainly you are.' The thin man looked at him. 'Brother's keeper. You're responsible.'

'Fruitcake,' Grissom said. 'I'm not responsible for anything. I could give a two-bit fart if you blew your brains out tomorrow.'

'Is that a fact.'

'That's right.'

'Then why didn't you leave me alone?'

'Oh boy,' Grissom said. 'You were hanging here. Christ, can't you see this thing from my side?' He clenched his fist and shook the thin man. 'Besides I didn't know you then.'

The thin man sniffed. 'You're selfish.'

'Oh sure. Selfish.'

'Yes, you are. You feel good for saving me. You can tell all your friends at the gym.' The thin man taunted. 'Selfish, selfish, selfish.'

'What do you know about the gym?' Grissom said. 'You don't know. And I didn't save you.'

'His brother's keeper,' the thin man said.

'Christ almighty.'

The thin man flapped his arms. Nearby the startled pigeon shit. Its white excrement streamed like saliva from one spar to the next, disappearing finally, because of the wind, into the crowd along the bank.

The thin man trembled with mirth. 'The mark of heavenly favour,' he said. The cords of his scrawny neck jumped beneath his skin as he turned hard little eyes to study Grissom. 'Fall from the sky among the rabble. Spattered like birdshit on the shoes of the curious.' He looked again at the crowd staring upwards. Their faces were pale as flower petals in the dusk.

'You'd fall in the water,' Grissom said.

'Blub, blub,' said the thin man.

'They'd have you out in two minutes.'

'Blubbity-blub.'

'Shit.' Grissom ground his teeth. He wanted to leave. It was Thursday. He'd planned on making spaghetti for supper. His son would be home from school already, and probably had that damn dog in the living room. He groaned. He could feel the coarse material prying his fingernails away from their beds. He realized he would have to change hands quickly, maintaining his balance on the beam while securing a new purchase on his load.

The thin man laughed out loud.

'Fat chance,' he giggled, anticipating Grissom's intention. He nodded at a pigeon that strutted nervously along the nearby spar. 'Hee, hee. Consider flying. Consider the feathered bird.'

'Shut up,' Grissom said. By now they could hear the police siren yowp in circular screams. The sound spun around the thin man's feet and disappeared into the sky.

'Fly, fly,' the thin man said. '"I caught this morning morning's minion, kingdom of daylight's dauphin, dapple-dawn-drawn Falcon ..."'

'Jesus,' Grissom said.

'That's him.' The thin man snickered. 'That's the guy, all right. Jesus, that high-flyer, "rung upon the rein of a wimpling wing" –'

'Oh boy,' Grissom said. '"Wimpling wing."'

The police car stopped next to the park below the bridge. Grissom watched the flat caps of the policemen move through the crowd. Presently the two uniformed men sought footholds in the sandy slope, climbing crablike, it seemed to Grissom, towards the trestle.

The thin man saw the uniforms. 'It's not fair,' he sulked. 'My heart in hiding stirred for a bird. A bird in the hand deserves a push.'

'Don't think I haven't considered it,' Grissom said.

'Then do it.'

'I can't.'

'Can't? Or won't? Chicken.' The thin man spat. 'Chicken hard heart. You're responsible.'

'Don't say that.'

'You're responsible.'

'If you aren't responsible,' the thin man snorted, 'then who is?'

Grissom tried to feel his fingers. The cloth now had no texture. It became a numb extension of his sleeping arm. He tried to squeeze his fingers tighter, but they wouldn't respond. His hand was a claw, a hook.

The thin man bit his lip and hung silently. He told Grissom: 'I'll never leave you, you know. I'll always be in your hand.'

'Don't be stupid.'

'It's true. Hours, days, months – *years* after this you'll feel me hanging from your arm. I'll hang there forever, a sort of millstone. A sort of albatross.'

'You'll be in the bughouse.'

'Well, yes,' the man agreed sadly. He started to sniffle. 'You've no idea what it's like in there.' He shook his head. 'But I won't leave your hand, no sir. I'll come back, sometimes – when you're eating, or trying to sleep, or making love – bingo – goodbye contentment, hello anguish, I'll be there.'

'Like hell,' Grissom said uneasily. 'The minute they cart you away you'll be yesterday's news.'

'No, I won't. The thin man flapped his arms again. The pigeon teetered forward, thrusting its head beyond the beam on which it was perched. Grissom saw its knuckled feet flatten as it tensed for flight, smelled the mustiness of its feathers.

'You're not a bird,' he told the thin man.

'I've heard that one before.'

'You can't just take off if you want to. People can't do that.'

'Says who.'

'Nobody has to say it, for crying out loud.'

The thin man scowled. 'I have free will. Free will, thank God and flappity-flap. And neither God nor I tolerate screw-ups.'

'You screwed yourself up.'

'No, I didn't,' the thin man said. 'Brother's keeper screwed up. And brother's keeper must pay the price.'

'Who's paying?' Grissom said. 'I don't know you, you don't know me.' He lowered his voice. 'If you want some interesting information, I don't even like you.'

The pigeon flew away. Grissom chose that moment to attempt a change of hands, but the thin man twisted his body back and forth, pirouetting in his overcoat so that Grissom had to hang on.

'Flappity, flappity, flappity,' the thin man sang.

'Cut it out,' Grissom said. The policemen still struggled up the slope. Pale gravel fell away from under their feet. Little hour glasses trickled beneath the policemen's boots.

'Your fingers are tired,' the thin man said.

'They're not tired.'

'You're sweating, did you know that? A drop of sweat dropped off your nose onto my shirt.'

'So what?'

'So I thought you were weeping for me.' The thin man wept. 'I thought you were Christ Our Lord.'

'Oh boy. Knock it off. This is all I need, the loony stuff. Knock it off. I'm not God, I don't believe in God, and if you want to make things a lot easier you'll keep away from the loony stuff. I'm no good at it.'

'Have mercy, Lord,' the thin man sobbed. 'Mercy, mercy, make me free.'

'Stop crying,' Grissom said. 'Stop crying. It'll turn out all right.'

'Promises,' the thin man said. 'Always broken promises.'

Grissom imagined letting go of the thin man, imagined the thin man twirling daintily, growing smaller and smaller until the dark water swallowed him. It could happen. Things like that happened.

'Listen,' Grissom confessed to the thin man. 'I work out to stay healthy. I have a kid. Okay, so maybe you don't – look, I believe in living. Know what I mean?'

'Living,' the thin man said.

'Okay,' Grissom said. 'So what's worth dying for, anyway?

You haven't told me that yet. What's worth dying for?'

'Flying is worth dying for,' the thin man said.

They listened to the running footsteps of the policemen on the trestle's planking.

'I'm sorry,' Grissom told the thin man.

'I bet.' The thin man cried freely now: oily tears dribbled from his chin. To Grissom the thin man's snuffling worked itself into a cadence with the sound of the policemen's boots, until the rasping, overtaxed breath of the winded cops transmuted the sounds into one.

Both policemen were overweight. With some difficulty they hauled the thin man up to the catwalk of the trestle. The thin man had taken to sobbing, sucking in his breath with a shivering noise, as though he had been caught unaware by a cold draught. His overcoat lay in a puddle around his knees. He rocked back and forth, holding his face in his hands.

'Never fly now,' he whimpered. 'Never not no.' He peered at Grissom through his skinny fingers. 'Never no,' he said. 'Gash gold-vermilion.'

'It's not up to me,' Grissom said, looking away.

'Never, never,' the thin man wailed. 'Fall gall flappity-flappity. Gone, gone long long gone.' He hunched his emaciated shoulders around his ears.

'You okay?' a policeman asked Grissom. Grissom nodded. The cop tipped his hat in the thin man's direction. 'Poor old bugger.' He raised his voice to the thin man. 'Take it easy, sir; take it easy now.'

The two constables bent down and hooked the thin man under the arms and dragged him along the catwalk. The thin man drooped between them, an effigy of himself. His feet bumped the spaces between the planks. Grissom massaged his shoulder and stared vacantly after the figures retreating into the gloom.

Bumpity-bump went the thin man's feet.

'Hey,' Grissom called, and flexed his stiffening arm. 'Hey, go easy on him, okay?'

The thin man's feet bumped hollowly.
'Hey! Wait a minute. Hold on for a second –'
From between his two escorts the thin man howled.

Per Ardua ad Astra

IN THE FALL of that year when the last letter arrived, Grissom was lying under the bench press in Cormy's Gym where he worked part time as a weight-training instructor. He hadn't expected any more letters – still less had he expected any message to be hand-delivered. All the other correspondence had come through the regular mail (the asylum's return address stamped in the upper left-hand corner), so it was a surprise when the messenger stepped in off the street.

In his torn tennis shoes and ruined face, the messenger resembled a resurrected angel, a back-alley survivor. He carried the envelope in one hand, and twirled his baseball cap on the other.

'Hey,' he said. 'You Grissom?'

'Why be formal, call me Jim.' Grissom swung up from under the barbell.

The messenger gauged his size. 'You don't look so big.'

'I don't remember claiming to be.'

'He said you were big.'

'Maybe I just looked that way from where he was. Who's he, anyway? Who are you?'

The messenger considered, as if this new possibility required a series of coloured slides to be projected inside his skull. Then he held out the envelope.

'Name's Mel. Mr Darwood says I'm supposed to stand here while you read it.'

'I'm not sure I want to read it.'

'He got your last letter. And your cheque. He sends you this.'

Grissom wiped his palms on his sweatpants. 'I don't know, Mel. I'm having second thoughts. Is Mr Darwood sure he wants to go through with this?'

'Is anybody sure about anything?'

'Is he sure about *this*?'

'He's willing to give it a shot.'

'Can I trust him?'

'Can he trust *you*?'

'What are we, Mel – rug traders?'

Mel showed what must have been teeth. 'Come on. Open it.'

Grissom read the letter. The handwriting was cramped, familiar, but unlike all the other letters this one held no poetry, no accusations, no pleas. *I have been released,* the letter said, *and I have decided you might be right. The business is still unsettled. Meet me today at the train trestle at four-thirty. Darwood*

'Well?' Mel put on his baseball cap and tugged at the brim. 'What should I tell him – yes or no?'

Grissom refolded the letter and put it in the envelope. 'Give me a minute, okay, Mel?'

'Sure. Listen, if it'll help, Mr D. says you can bring along your son.'

'Leave my son out of this.'

'Mr D. feels pretty bad, you know.'

'Just leave my son out of this.'

'All right. Okay.' Mel opened his hands. 'So what's it going to be?'

Grissom considered. 'I'll be there.'

'Good.' Mel turned to go. 'Hey – you remember how to get there, don't you?'

'I remember,' Grissom said.

SEVEN MONTHS BEFORE, Grissom, in pursuit of nothing more complicated than good health, had been jogging through Riversdale Park where he happened to see – just happened, pure chance! – skinny Darwood leap from one of the girders of the Tenth Street train trestle. (The trestle, an ancient geometric jumble of blackened steel, spanned the river where the current ran particularly fast and deep. In a city known for its bridges, the trestle was a favourite haunt of morose lovers and ambitious suicides.)

On that day Darwood's ambition was thwarted, however: his

overcoat snagged on a bridge spar and left him dangling seventy feet above the river, his legs thrashing – a signal to Grissom to climb up there and do something.

So Grissom climbed, and spent the next half hour struggling to hang on to Darwood who, it turned out, was feisty and wiry and obdurately determined to fall from the bridge one way or another. Grissom fisted the old man's overcoat in his right hand and settled in for a wrestling match that was both physical and verbal. Darwood kicked and gouged and spat; he drifted in and out of lucidity and nonsense; he wanted to fly. 'I caught this morning morning's minion,' he told Grissom. 'Dapple-dawn drawn Falcon. Jesus, that high-flier, rung upon the rein of a wimpling wing.' At first Grissom paid little attention, and judged the old man to be a simple loony, as batty as a bachelor uncle. But as time went on Grissom saw something other than craziness in the old man's eyes.

A desperation was there and a pleading, which reminded Grissom of the small and wounded birds he'd once tried to nurse back to health when he was a kid. It was not so much death as freedom the old man wanted.

Even so, Grissom had hung on until the police arrived. Darwood had insulted, cajoled and begged him for release. Admitting he had no family or friends, the old man at one point started to cry. 'My heart stirred for a bird,' he wept. 'A bird in the hand deserves a push. Let me go.'

But Grissom would not. As he explained to Darwood, 'I believe in living.'

A statement worthy of a simple man with simple values, or so said the newspapers who played out the story on their front pages after Darwood had been safely stowed in the Eastview Centre for the Emotionally Disturbed. Grissom the reporters presented as a man of Herculean strength and similar intellect, a single-parent father whose self-effacement concealed, among other things, a big heart. However true such claims might have been, and however tempted Grissom was to believe them, he remained taciturn during interviews, and photographs revealed his face to be unusually glum for that of a publicized hero. In his silence Grissom brooded that heroism was at best shallow and gratuitous, the people should mind their own business, and that in light of Darwood's arguments and the events that happened after it, would have been better if Grissom had simply let the little man go.

Why? – Because that afternoon, while he was defending the cause of life and straining an already sore elbow it just so happened – just happened, pure chance! – that his ten-year-old son Clayton came home early from school, dumped his book bag on the front porch and sprinted – sprinted, without looking! – across the street to the neighbour's to get the spare house key. And ran smack into a Tastemaster bread van driven by a pouchy-eyed driver named Lewis who hadn't had an accident in twenty-three years.

For Grissom, a simple man with simple values, the finger of culpability for his son's accident pointed directly at himself. It was only later when the boy's condition was fully diagnosed that he wondered if the finger pointed at Darwood as well.

Yet he visited them both, divided his time between them. Each night he spent with his son; but on Sundays he wheeled up the curving tree-lined drive to the Eastview Centre, and in the visitors' room, or on a sunny bench overlooking the grounds, he met with Darwood.

'Hey Mr D., how they treating you?'

The old man would shrink against a wall or the far end of the bench, suspicious in his institutional clothes. 'Is your mind a mountain? Can you fathom your thoughts?'

'I like the PJ's Mr D. No kidding, they go with the walls here. But what would you say if I brought you something with a little more colour – something with stripes, maybe?'

Darwood hugged himself and wept; Grissom put an arm around his shoulders. 'Come on, Mr D. What do I know about wardrobes?' When the old man sagged against him, it seemed to Grissom that Mr Darwood was no meatier than Clayton who lay in the hospital wide awake, bony and vulnerable in the dark.

The visits continued throughout the summer. Darwood grew more and more lucid. He noticed the pigeons on the path; pointed out the patterns of the hospital routine.

One day in July he admitted that he'd been told Grissom's son had been injured. 'And here I have pitied my poor Jackself, pitied tormented mind tormenting yet.'

'No need for poetry, Mr D. Or torment or pity for that matter.' Though it was what Grissom wanted, he realized: a confession that might absolve them both.

But Darwood grabbed Grissom's shirtfront and pressed his face close. 'I cast for comfort I can no more get than blind eyes in their dark can day.'

'Well, Jesus, Mr Darwood, if you're sorry just say so.'

'Or thirst can find thirst's all-in-all in all a world of wet.'

'Let go now, Mr D.'

'Beauty-in-the-ghost!' Mr Darwood cried, clinging. 'Deliver it, early now, long before death; give beauty, beauty, beauty back to God!'

'Well, shit,' Grissom said, and pushed the old man from him more roughly than he intended.

Of course the hospital staff advised Grissom to stay away. They accepted his letters when he sent them, even though Grissom was never sure if Darwood had read them all. What did he say in those letters, anyway? What confessions, accusations did he make to a man whose mind he *couldn't* fathom? *Dear Mr Darwood,* he wrote, *If we're going to get anywhere in this thing, you'll have to knock off the poetry ... Dear Mr Darwood, I don't see how you can call what happened an act of faith. Jesus Christ, I told you before I don't believe ... Dear Mr Darwood, I just want to have an answer for Clayton. Sure, maybe you're right, maybe 'Prayer shall fetch pity eternal', but I ask you: who needs eternal pity anyway? My boy just wants to know why such things happen. He can't walk, see, and he wants to know why.*

In a state of confusion, guilt and accusation, Grissom started to write the letters. To his surprise, Darwood answered them.

ON HIS WAY to the train trestle that afternoon, Grissom stopped off at the hospital where he took the elevator up to the children's ward. When he arrived at Clayton's room he found the boy awake.

'I thought you were supposed to nap in the afternoons.'

'I don't have to. I got itchy and I couldn't sleep. I'm too old to nap anyway.' Clayton raised his thin white arms and let them fall. The only parts of his son's body that Grissom had seen since the accident were the arms, face and feet. The rest lay encased in a body cast from ankles to chin. A hip had been crushed and hadn't healed properly, and there was still much speculation about the boy's spine, which had undergone two separate operations. 'We'll leave the second cast on,' the surgeon had said, 'until we're sure.' Since then Clayton had lain rigidly at attention, like a rusted Tin Man. His face was pale, his blond hair almost white. Sometimes Grissom thought of his son as a cocoon or chrysalis. A metamorphosis was taking place under the plaster and gauze; it might astonish him, if only Grissom could see it.

'Did Dr. Sobotka check on you today?'

'This morning. He poked my toes and stuff.'

'And?'

'I don't know.'

'What do you mean you don't know? Did you feel anything or not?'

'I don't *know*. With everybody poking at me all the time I can't *tell* any more. Maybe I felt something. I don't *know*.'

'Okay. All right. Take it easy.' Grissom laid his hand on his son's arm. 'Where were you itchy?'

'The same place. On my chest.'

'Why didn't you use the snake?' Grissom glanced around the room for the scratcher he'd fashioned out of a coat-hanger and adhesive tape.

'The Butch took it away from me.'

'Don't call her the Butch.'

'*You* were the one that called her the Butch first.'

'That was before. And anyway it's not me who has to live here.

If I had to live here, I sure wouldn't call her the Butch.'

In fact, for a while after his son's accident, Grissom *had* lived at the hospital. The Butch, an efficient ward nurse with short hair and broad shoulders, had allowed Grissom to set up a cot in Clayton's room. 'It's okay with Dr. Sobotka, so it's okay with me,' she said. 'But I'll warn you now. One hint of interference and you're out of here.' The Butch was an avid hiker and rock-climber. 'Just keep an eye on him,' she confided. 'Watch for any sign of movement, or feeling. Above all, try to keep his spirits up. I've seen lots of spinal injuries. Sometimes, when morale is high –' She smiled, leaving Grissom to consider the miraculous.

Which he did, for the first week or two. At night he lay awake beside his son waiting for something to happen. Asleep, Clayton was a lip-smacker, a teeth-grinder, an occasional mumbler whose nocturnal ramblings Grissom interpreted as dream games of frozen tag and street hockey, cops-and-robbers, or prisoner's base. Physical himself, Grissom painted his son in the same colours. In Grissom's estimation whole careers Clayton might have pursued went up in flames. Gone were the dreams of champion boxer, gymnast, jazz dancer, NHL hockey star. (It was useless to point out that the boy showed little potential in any of these directions – was, after all, simply a normal active boy but hardly Olympic material. Useless, too, to tell Grissom such things. Grissom hadn't been born strong; he'd built himself that way, and only divorce and incipient middle age had pushed him into the struggle against vindictive gravity.) Lying beside Clayton in the hospital, he had entertained hopeful if illogical notions that strength, spirit, and other notable traits could bridge the narrow gap between cot and bed, and through mysterious osmosis restore the boy's health and will to live.

A vain hope, perhaps, but Grissom was a gambler. Unreligious, at times flirting with existentialist flapdoodle (After all, what meaning could he find in his son's running full tilt into a moving bread truck? What purpose was there in a ten-year-old snapping his spine as casually as some people crack chicken bones?) – Grissom nonetheless anticipated (with all an atheist's irrational fervour) a Gesture from God. Give him his boy back whole and in working order and Grissom would dedicate his redundant strength to some worthy, legitimate fund-raising cause: famine, Amnesty International, the Beluga whale. Months had passed, however, and still the boy's toes protruded from his cast as featureless and numb as canned hams.

'Did you get the book?' Clayton asked.

'No, I forgot. I'll pick it up later today. The librarian told me on Tuesday it would be in today. She says the *Titanic* is a hot item these days.' Grissom's son, having lived through his own disaster, had grown fascinated by others. The Great Fire of London, Hiroshima, the San Francisco Earthquake – these were his reading materials.

'The kid's morbid,' Grissom told the Butch the first time he'd staggered in under an armload of disaster books.

'Wouldn't you be?' Despite her crewcut and sensible hands, the Butch had a smile that did something to her eyes, and a back-side Grissom admired. Divorced for two years, he had began to notice that beauty turned up in unexpected places.

'Hey,' he told his son. 'I got a new one for you.'

'Who cares.'

'Come on, don't be like that. We can make it for money this time.'

The boy's eyes relented. 'Okay.' He sat up; that is, his eye-brows rose and his chin appeared to lift. Immobility had pro-vided Clayton with a new set of body expressions, mostly facial.

'Here it is: *A mari usque ad mare.*'

'Aw, that's easy. From sea to sea. Canada's motto.'

'Right. One for you.' Grissom fished a quarter out of his pocket and laid it on the bed table.

Clayton lay back, thinking. '*Todo por la patria,*' he said finally.

'Spanish.'

'Spanish what?'

'Give me a minute.' Grissom rubbed his nose. 'All for the country.'

'And –?'

'Motto of –' Grissom struggled. 'Motto of – the Spanish mon-archy.'

'Wrong. Guardia Civil. That's a dime. Okay, give me another one.'

'*Per ardua ad astra.*'

The boy scowled, pursed his lips. 'I know this one ... *Per ardua ad astra.*' He crossed his hands over his chest. Slender, with oval nailbeds, Clayton's hands resembled those of his mother, a woman who'd gone on to another marriage and other children. Grissom found himself wishing for a moment that his son hadn't inherited those sensitive, slender fingers.

'Royal Canadian Air force,' Clayton said. 'Isn't it?'

'That's right. You've got your dime back. But what's it mean?'

'Something – something to the stars.'

'Close, but still only a dime.'

Clayton closed his eyes. Lying thus, he made Grissom fearful. 'Come on, Clayton.'

The boy opened his eyes. 'Through adversity to the stars.' He gazed at Grissom. 'Oh, puke.'

'It's not puke.'

'I thought we weren't going to use crap like that.'

'Watch your language.' Grissom folded his hands between his knees. 'Give me one.'

Clayton lay back. 'I don't think so. I'm tired.'

Grissom stood and poured them both glasses of water. 'I heard from Darwood today.'

'I don't want to hear another letter.'

'This one's different.'

'All that poetry and crap. I don't know what he's talking about. I don't even know *him*, Dad.'

Grissom put a straw in his son's water and handed the glass over. 'He's been released. He must be cured. That's when they release them, you know – when they're cured.'

'I don't want to hear about it. Please, Dad. I know what we said but I don't want to hear about it. What difference does it make?'

'It makes a difference.' Grissom took a breath. 'Anyway, you won't have anything to do with it. He's going to see me. Just me.'

Clayton turned away.

He can't even turn his head, Grissom thought. Only his eyes.

'You don't have to do it, Dad.'

'You don't have to tell me what I don't have to do.' Grissom's tongue felt thick. He sat down again. After a while he pulled the covers from the foot of the bed and tickled the soles of his son's feet.

'I can't feel anything,' Clayton said, and started to cry.

The Butch came in, carrying juice on a tray. 'What's with you guys?' Her real name, the one on her name tag, was Marion. She looked at them both, put down the tray and tucked the blankets around Clayton's feet. Efficiency and optimism animated her. Grissom saw that what he'd thought was callousness was really self-defence: a heart took a risk being worn on a sleeve. Marion knew that.

'You guys, you guys.' She shook her head gently. 'These things take time – don't you know that? Didn't I tell you that already?'

THE SUN had already faded when Grissom drove into the parking lot overlooking the river. Across the water the park lay bathed in a queer orange light, as if illuminated through smoke. Grissom stepped out of the car and into the autumn air. A chill wind carried the scent of fallen leaves and snow. At the end of the parking lot where the gravel petered out, Mel the messenger stood expectantly. Behind him loomed the bridge pylons, massive concrete wedges with feet in the water and heads in the sky. Above, the steel girders and railway tracks hung impossibly high in the air.

'Hey, Mel. Where's Mr Darwood?'

Mel raised an arm upward in a gesture that might've been a benediction. Grissom looked up: Darwood's thin figure in its familiar tweed overcoat leaned over the parapet. In an anxious moment of *déjà vu* Grissom imagined the old man falling; imagined Darwood jumping; imagined himself grabbing Darwood by the collar and the seat of the pants and heaving him, bouncer-style, head first off the bridge.

Grissom clambered up the bank, slipping in the gravel while pigeons exploded on whirring wings from under the girders. Halfway up he stopped among shrivelled clover and knapweed to wipe sweat from his throbbing forehead. He tried to recall what had been said in the letters he and Darwood had exchanged. *You said if I didn't let you go I would be responsible for you, and while that's true it's my opinion that you are responsible too, Mr Darwood. You can argue any way you want, but if I hadn't bothered to pull you off the bridge Clayton wouldn't be crippled today. That's what it all boils down to.*

'The world is charged with the grandeur of God,' Mr Darwood had quoted.

Knock off the Hopkins, Mr Darwood. I've read his poetry and while it's fine as poetry it doesn't change things. We're responsible for Clayton. We put him where he is. You and me.

'The grandeur of God will flame out, like shining from shook foil.'

Don't write to me about foil, I'm not interested in foil.

'The Holy Ghost over the bent World broods with warm breast and ah! bright wings.'

To hell with wings.

Annoyed now, Grissom scrambled the last few feet up to the tracks where the gravel had been smudged by the exhaust of passing trains.

Straightening, he paused to gaze vertiginously down at the water, which was flecked with yellow foam and dotted by gulls and refuse. The gaps between the ties yawned at each step, and if he were looking for an epiphany, he'd probably found at least one: train trestles are scary. He stepped along the tracks as daintily as a tight-rope walker. The breeze shot quick draughts up his trousers.

What did I expect? he wondered.

Darwood waited with his hands in his pockets, poised on the edge of the bridge. He still looked wizened and his ancient face thrust out of his collar like a defiant fist. He gave Grissom the impression of a scrawny-necked bird about to squawk the uncensored truth, and although his eyes were still galvanized by the madness, something else shone there too.

'Brother's keeper,' Darwood said. 'Welcome home. The old place looks the same, does it not?'

'It seems higher this time, Mr D.'

'I might've said not high enough.' Darwood looked coyly away, on the verge of revelation. When he turned back again, he was smiling. 'The cheque was very thoughtful, very generous.'

'I figured you could use some money once you got out.'

'And guilt? Did you figure I could use that too?'

Grissom shrugged. 'It seemed a shame to keep it all to myself.'

'"No worst there is none", eh? "Pitched past pitch of grief", are we?'

'He can't walk, Mr Darwood. He's ten years old.'

Darwood nodded. The wind lifted his hair in wisps. '" The mind has mountains, no-man fathomed",' he admitted. '"All life death does end and each day dies with sleep."' He gazed down at the water, his figure fixed like a question mark against the sky, until something – a bluster of wind – roused him, so that he shuffled nervously from one foot to the other. 'We're back where we started, aren't we?'

Grissom had his hands in his pockets. 'Yes, we are.'

'Well.' Mr Darwood sidestepped towards the edge. 'Let's get on with it.'

LATER WHEN GRISSOM tried to recall the details of that after-noon – the way the light reflected off the water, the first sting of falling snow, the freckles that dotted Mr Darwood's thin-haired skull as Grissom lowered him over the side of the bridge – he found the specifics eluded him. He could recall hitching Mr Darwood's overcoat over the bridge spar, but not the texture of the overcoat's cloth. He could remember releasing Mr Dar-wood's collar, surrendering the old man's weight to the bridge, but he couldn't say at what precise moment he had let go.

'But how did you know, Dad?' Clayton interrupted his father's telling. 'How did you know he wouldn't jump?'

'I just knew,' Grissom said.

But he hadn't known. Darwood had wriggled and pitched on the bridge spar like a hooked fish, to the encouragement of Mel the messenger who waved his angel arms below. ' "No, I'll not carrion comfort, Despair, not feast on thee",' Darwood had yelled at one point, frightening Grissom, for whom poetry belonged in books. Relenting, Grissom had moved to pull the victim in, until he realized the wiry old man's contortions were really scissor-legged gymnastics intended to preserve life, not end it. Huffed, blown, skinned on knees and elbows, Darwood had finally crawled up on the bridge deck and when he'd regained his breath admitted that he'd never try that again.

'We're even,' he'd said, accepting an arm from the solicitous Grissom. 'I've wrestled with my God.'

Cold comfort to a ten-year-old whose legs didn't work. But it was the best Grissom could offer his son until, several months into the winter, a third operation restored some of the feeling in the boy's legs – enough so that the knees, like thin marionette's limbs, could bend. Then Grissom, who embraced nurse Marion over-long and over-fervently, felt the tremendous blossoming of – of what? – not a miracle certainly, but something very much like one. Amazement perhaps, or gratitude for the generosity and justice that sometimes attend struggle.

'Oh, puke, that sounds like poetry,' Clayton said.

And Grissom, pleased, conceded that it did.

Blue Husbands

1. BURTON FIRST SAW her at the gymnasium where her husband died. The husband was a paunchy real estate agent who came in three times a week to skip rope until his sweatshirt stuck between his shoulder blades. One Wednesday he launched his final flurry of 'crossovers', a difficult skipping manoeuvre which reminded Burton of tap-dancing. The real estate man tap-danced for two minutes, turned blue and fell down.

Cormy and Grissom, the gym owners, worked on the dying man's heart. Between cardiopulmonary jolts Cormy suggested that someone telephone the man's wife, and handed Burton a card. So Burton phoned and said *Your husband's in trouble, he's collapsed,* and she said, *My God, I'll be right over.*

Her name was Elaine Francis. She'd been married to the real estate man for twenty-six years.

Of course the couple was whisked away in the ambulance, the husband being the colour he was. Before the ambulance doors slammed shut, Burton glimpsed Elaine Francis's strong hand stroking her fallen mate's forehead. She was a round-busted, wide-hipped woman, swarthy and fifty – in Burton's estimation, of a size and age to appreciate the keenness of desolation. She looked Greek or Italian, and Burton could imagine her in black, honouring her husband in some far-off piazza, trudging daily to the cathedral where she'd light candles until grief – or too much pasta – swelled her ankles. Watching her stroke her husband's forehead he decided dignity was what she'd be after: sincerity, praise for her courage and loyalty. In return, she'd be grateful. In Burton's opinion, the ones with the strong hands were always grateful. They'd had to endure.

He went to the funeral.

The service was well attended. At the cemetery the real estate man's last rites took on the festiveness of an open-house; a crowd of his competitors showed up, jaunty in their bright company jackets. The day itself was dismal, misted by a fine drizzle which beaded the gravestones and dripped from the trees, but the real estate people clustered to one side of the grave and murmured, as if they were appraising a property and weren't quite sure their colleague hadn't been burned on his last big land deal.

Gravediggers had draped a fluorescent orange tarp over the mound to keep it dry, and the plastic flared behind the mourners like a bonfire. With her back to it, Elaine Francis stood between her two grown-up sons like someone trying to keep warm.

When all the words had been spoken and the coffin lowered, Burton joined the queue to offer his condolences. 'He'll be missed,' he said, swallowing hard as he cradled her hand in his.

'Yes.' She looked him full in the face. 'You knew him then?'

'At Cormy's Gym. I was the one who telephoned.'

'Yes.' She nodded. 'Of course.' There was grace to her neck and her large hazel eyes were flecked with motes of light. Her two sons stood tall on either side.

'Yes,' she said again. 'I remember. Thank you. Thank you for coming.' And gazing at him steadily, she winked.

Burton turned away and stumbled across the soggy leaves to his car. He was no expert, but a wink was a wink – wasn't it? In his mind he flipped through his meagre catalogue of winks: the long slow sly; the half-speed deadpan; the brief crinkle; the twinkle.

Maybe that was it. Maybe her hazel eyes (with freckles of light – eccentric, they now seemed to him, possibly freakish – though that was harsh) had merely twinkled. But who twinkled at funerals? Murderers? Adulteresses? Ghouls? This woman was none of those. Still the wink, if wink it was, demanded explanation.

Perhaps she mistook him for someone else, an old friend to whom she could signal a comradely 'I'm-all-right-Jack' without the protocol of mourning. Or perhaps – he eased himself behind the wheel and turned the ignition key – perhaps she suffered from some eye disorder, some opthalmological distress that involved the deterioration of the wink nerves to a point where

they fired indiscriminately during public functions such as wed-
dings and funerals. If such were the case, her life must have been
plagued by her feverish, inadvertent winking, and legions of pri-
ests, Scout troop leaders and bank managers had writhed exqui-
sitely under the illusion that she had silently propositioned them.

On the other hand, he thought, as he drove back to his office,
maybe he'd imagined the whole thing and had seen the wink
precisely because it wasn't there, precisely because he'd wanted
to see it. His fascination with widows was well developed by this
time; maybe winking widows were the next step in its escalation.

2. PUT IT THIS WAY: Burton's wife had run off with a heart
surgeon. Burton knew the guy – one of the neighbourhood regulars who didn't let a much-publicized medical reputation stop
him from inviting a select few over for a pool party, Japanese
food (catered), and drinks in the dusky evening to the strains of
old rock 'n' roll and progressive jazz. The surgeon was a tall man
with a smile and slender fingers. Naturally Burton's wife, Celia,
a former nurse, talked to the doctor about anginas and triple
by-pass surgery. In the course of so many detailed anatomical
conversations one thing must've led to another. Albert – for so
the medical man insisted on being called, the implication being
he was connected in an obscure way to Schweitzer – apparently
fell for Celia's ticker; he made valentine overtures, and won it.

Sometimes in the middle of the night Burton wondered if the
surgeon hadn't seen enough hearts day after day. Hadn't he
fondled enough ventricles, squeezed enough aortas to keep him
satisfied? Like Burton, the surgeon was married with children.
He was a blue husband, and his furtive couplings with Celia
shattered so many hearts that the resultant gore rivalled that of
the horror-movie videos that Burton's teen-aged kids now
watched on the heart surgeon's colour TV.

All this Burton spilled to his brother the day Burton's divorce
became final.

'I was a blue husband too,' Burton said into his beer. The bar
they sat in overlooked the harbour.

His brother shook his head. He was a dentist, burdened by wisdom. He looked into people's mouths and read their souls: gums told a lot about a person. 'Christ, blue husbands. Have you any idea how much I hated it when the old man talked like that? He had the whole institution of marriage reduced to a paintbox.'

The senior Burton had been an unrepentant philanderer. Short, jovial, with no hair and big forearms, he'd been a commercial traveller unbothered by clichés. 'I'm the travelling salesman they tell jokes about,' he liked to say. His married life had been littered with waitresses, salesgirls and hotel maids. 'I was a blue husband,' he admitted on his deathbed. 'Your mother never recognized my true colour.'

Burton senior had decided that husbands – like cars and argyle socks – came in different colours.

'First you've got your earthtone husbands. They're the guys that never talk or if they do it's to yap about crabgrass or the weather. Then you got your red husbands, I don't mean commies I mean fireballs, the guys that're always madder 'n hell and want to hit people. Then you've got your black husbands, the guys with hearts the colour of soot, who spend ten years brooding over something petty before they finally get up one morning and brain their wife with an axe. Out in left field you've got your green husbands, the ones who just want to grow. But you've got to be careful. Green husbands got to be cared for. They can turn blue overnight.' The old man considered himself a green husband who'd been nipped by marital frost – a greener gone blue.

'The old man,' Burton's brother said, 'was boundless in his hypocrisy. It's a wonder mother never poisoned him.'

'She forgave him in the end.'

'Big deal, he was dead.'

'Love is strange.'

'Is that how you explain this widow business?' Burton's brother asked. 'I've been told you went to Larry Francis's funeral and drooled all over his widow's hand.'

'She winked at me.'

'Pardon me?'

'Like this.'

'Elaine Francis winked at you at her husband's funeral?'

'I don't know what else to call it.'

'Jesus Christ,' Burton's brother said.

'I think it was a wink.'

'Ah.' Burton's brother cocked his balding head to one side. 'Ah. You think. Let me tell you what *I* think. I think you've pushed this widow thing too far. I think you're near the edge. You haven't been answering any ads lately, have you? You said you were going to give up the ads.'

'I gave up the ads.'

'So now you're dipping into the obituaries for dates?'

'I knew Larry Francis. I was there when he collapsed. I was the one who called his – Elaine.'

Burton's brother shook his head. 'This is probably a phobia of some kind. Jesus. The other day Celia phoned me up and said you've been spying on her.'

'I have not.'

'She said you park outside her house at night and stare.'

'I'm checking on the kids.'

'You should check on yourself. Go see a doctor, for God's sake.'

But Burton didn't want to see a doctor. He wanted to see widows; had, in fact, seen quite a few of them since his separation. After he'd said goodbye to his wife and kids and the house they'd all lived in, he'd moved into a bachelor apartment with chrome furniture, a rowing machine, and a black-and-white TV. He went into mourning and who better to share grief with than widows?

Widows, he discovered, recognized him as a loner. They were patient and understanding. Having had something taken from them, they were willing to give. Their strength astonished him. Mere infidelity hadn't stolen their loved ones: the Grim Reaper had.

He read their ads in the classifieds:

Widow, 52, interested in music, tennis. Seeks companionship of man 45-50. Non-smoker.

Widow, 47, seeks male companionship. Box 670 this paper. No triflers please.

He wrote to them. Sometimes they met, and Burton took them to a restaurant, a movie, the zoo. He played squash with them, walked their dogs, pushed their carts through supermarkets. Over apple pie and wedges of cheese he congratulated them on their homes and their children, cursed their shyster lawyers and heartless relatives. Adaptable, he was anything a widow wanted him to be – confidant, guest, friend. Not lover, however. Burton drew the line at sex.

And what a humiliating line it was. Have a widow suggest sex and Burton grew coy. Suggest (as one lively widow Rosemary did) that sleeping together might not be love but it was a fairly convincing substitute, and Burton headed for the door, mouth dry, palms sweating.

It wasn't ethics exactly. It wasn't health exactly – although the new sexual diseases had Burton guessing about pre-copulation diplomacy. (How, for instance, was he supposed to broach the subject of blood tests and still maintain a romantic zeal?) It wasn't even a matter of sexual vanity exactly, for although Celia had been his only sexual partner throughout his married life, Burton felt reasonably confident that given the right circumstances he'd have enough sap to rise to the occasion with a stranger. No, what prevented Burton from falling into the grateful arms of a willing widow was the fear that at the critical moment of the union, when he and the widow were irredeemably socketed together, she'd look into his eyes and see that he was a fraud.

Why? Why was he a phony? Why were the widows good to him, why did they take him to their tables, their bosoms, their photograph albums? Why couldn't they see in him the blue husband he really was – not a widower at all, but a blue husband who parked on the dark street outside his divorced family's new home, just to make sure the doors were locked, the dogs were in, and the kids' light was out by 10:30? Why couldn't these widows see he was a trifler, a dilettante?

Because Burton lied to them, that's why.

He told them he was widowed too.

3. TWO WEEKS AFTER the funeral Elaine Francis showed up at Cormy's Gym, dressed in her husband's grey sweatsuit. 'Larry had a three-year membership here. It seemed a shame to waste it.'

She said this unwinkingly. Burton searched her freckled green eyes for what he'd come to think of as a secret sign. When she gave none, he noticed the rest of her.

She wasn't svelte. Her husband's sweats, too long, fitted her latitudinally. Exposed by rolled-up sleeves, her famous hands thickened at the wrists and swelled into substantial forearms. She was compact, more muscular than fat. She held her chin high, which made her neck graceful; her head was round and neat. Her jaw was firm, her lips full: power and beauty fought for control of her. There was a lushness about her, too, a subterranean sensuality that emanated from her compactness.

Burton decided she was one of the most erotic women he had ever met.

She told him she was trying to slim. Grissom, the instructor, had prescribed light weights and jogging three times a week. 'He suggested I run with you through the park and along the seawall. If it's not an imposition.'

'It's three miles.'

'That's all right.' She smiled. 'I think my heart's sounder than Larry's was.'

Burton wondered if she meant to be satirical.

'I usually run at four o'clock,' he said.

'Good. We can start today then.'

So three times a week they ran the cedar-chip paths through the park, then along the seawall that overlooked rusting freighters anchored in the bay. Gulls shrieked at their passing,

teenagers in spiky hair ignored them. Other more serious office
athletes smirked at their incongruity – Burton's giraffe-like
galumphing next to Elaine Francis's egg-beater shuffle. In the
silent way of runners they swapped information. She heard his
knees creak and took it easy on the hills. He watched her pound-
ing heels and allowed her the grassy verge beside the pavement.
After a half-dozen runs, they grew accustomed to each other's
raspings and spittle, and a vocational banter shaped their conversations.

'Don't you ever sweat? I've never seen you sweat.'

'Of course I sweat. Larry's suit soaks it up, that's all.'

'But you don't sweat like I sweat.'

'I don't run like you run.'

'That sounds like a criticism, Elaine.'

'A matter of semantics. If I ran like you run, I'd sweat like you
sweat. Providing I were you and you were me.'

'What you mean is you don't sweat.'

'What I mean is we each have our own way of sweating.'

'So you're an individualist?'

'I'm an individual. If you're interested in "ists" that's your
business.'

The fact is Burton got used to her. During their runs she
jogged beside him unflaggingly. He extrapolated this dogged-
ness to include the virtues of loyalty and determination, and
teetered dangerously on the brink of thinking of her as a Fine
Woman. He said little, however. Their intimacy had little to do
with words; rather, it grew out of shared exertion. After their
runs they lifted weights at Cormy's Gym: they became, as the
gym regulars put it, training partners. And as the weeks passed
Burton learned to anticipate Elaine's secret grunts and sighs.
The involuntary murmurs she released in mid-exercise sounded
to him like the keenings of love. He watched her strain under the
pulleys on the Universal machine, watched her skip the very rope
that had killed her husband. Under her sweatsuit she moved
through her exercise routine exactly as Burton did. He groaned
under the same pulleys, skipped the same rope. It was as though

their bodies, by duplicating breath, exertion, and release, moved in an empathetic ballet with one another. Sometimes Burton almost felt he *was* Elaine Francis. We're like a dancer, he thought, like one dancer and her shadow. The image stayed with him through the summer, and at times he felt sentimental about it – almost sappy.

'I miss Larry,' she told him once. 'But not in the way I thought I would. I thought I'd miss all the ordinary things, the things they write songs about – you know, the sound of his voice, the touch of his hand –'

'And don't you?'

'At first I did. But now I miss – I don't know – the *space* he occupied. The *heaviness* of him. It's so *empty* were Larry used to be.'

He wanted to ask her why she winked at him at the funeral then, if she felt so much. But instead he said, 'Yes, that's how it was when I lost Celia.'

Elaine Francis touched his arm. 'You know, you've never told me how she died.'

'Car crash.' Incredibly, Burton's eyes grew watery. 'On the freeway bridge. She and the girls died instantly.'

'Girls?'

'My daughters, Charlotte and Darlene.'

'I'm so sorry.'

So was Burton. He was confused, too. If he wanted comfort from his lie to Elaine Francis, he wasn't getting it. The widow business was getting more complicated than he'd imagined. Sometimes when he parked under the night-time trees in Celia's new neighbourhood, he had the peculiar sense that he was a ghost, watching real people live their lives. He saw his wife and daughters move with ease and familiarity past the windows of their new house, and his heart ached. In the clandestine front seat of his car, he marvelled that they didn't miss the space *he* had occupied, the heaviness of *him*.

Once a month Burton picked up his daughters and took them on drives or hikes out of the city, partly to get them far away from

Celia, but partly to avoid running into Elaine Francis. His daughters, who were thirteen and fifteen, grew weary of these monthly jaunts.

'Why can't we go to a movie once in a while, or a play?' Darlene, his eldest, wanted to know. 'What's so fascinating about this outdoor stuff all the time?'

'It's healthy!' Burton used his jolly voice when he was with his daughters. He barked at them jovially, as if they were on a hayride and he had to shout into the wind. 'It's good for you!'

'We're healthy *now*, Daddy.'

'I know that.'

'So why do you spy on us all the time? We're all right, Daddy. You don't have to *spy* on us.'

'I just like to make sure you're all right, that's all.'

To Burton's dismay his daughters appeared to have adjusted to their new life: even puberty hadn't presented them with any more than the usual annoyances and obstacles. Charlotte fretted over her braces and the size of her nose, but Darlene was there to lead her; and Celia was there too. The girls never complained about the new arrangement. Even so, Burton maintained his nightly vigil outside their house. Disaster played no favourites. Now and then in the newspaper he read about distraught fathers who kidnapped their children. He found himself sympathizing with those men, as if they all belonged to some crazed but legitimate fraternity.

Then, early in September, Celia phoned him and said if he didn't stop parking outside her house at night she was going to secure a restraining order against him. Why did he have to upset the girls by lurking like a common burglar on their street? On several occasions she'd had to stop Albert from coming down there and punching his lights out.

'Punching?' Burton said. 'Is that part of the Hippocratic oath?'

'It's not funny, Burton.' Like everyone else, Celia had always called him by his last name. 'The girls don't show it, but they're disturbed by this. They think Daddy's going crazy.'

'What do you think, Celia?'

'I don't know. I'm not sure I care. All I know is you have to stop spying on us. Stop it. Stop it.' Celia might've been crying, but over the phone Burton couldn't be sure. 'It's over, Burton, it's over. What's the matter with you anyway?'

4. ELAINE FRANCIS LIVED in a bungalow that overlooked the bay. From her kitchen window Burton could see the lights of the distant north shore shimmer across the water like party streamers. Beyond and above lay the hulking darkness of the mountains.

'Larry always claimed we bought this house for the view,' Elaine Francis said. 'But he wasn't above boasting to his real estate friends how little we paid for it.' She wore a dark skirt and a creamy blouse. Her movements in her own kitchen were sure and hospitable. The apron she wore said I Made It to Salmon-burger Saturday: one of her sons was in advertising. Under the kitchen lights she looked tanned and vigorous. She set Burton to work slicing tomatoes and mushrooms for the salad.

The supper included candlelight, two bottles of red wine, and a richly-sauced paella made with rabbit, chicken, and zingingly-spiced saffron rice which, after three helpings, seduced Burton into loosening his belt and waxing reminiscent. Over coffee and flan, he described for Elaine Francis his father's catalogue of the colours of husbands.

'Even while Celia was alive,' he confided, tipsy, 'I think I was becoming a blue husband.'

Interested, she leaned across the table. 'Did she know that?'

'I doubt it.'

'Then maybe you should tell her now. You can use my phone.'

He sipped his coffee, aware that you can't blame too much wine for everything. After a moment of what he hoped looked like intelligent deliberation, he asked how long she had known.

'A couple of weeks now. Your brother's my dentist.'

'Ah.'

'I thought you might've wanted to tell me yourself.'

'That would've been the honourable thing to do, all right.'

'But –?'

'But "I don't run like you run." Isn't that what you said?'

She studied him silently, her elbows on the table, her strong hands clasped in front of her. Then she got up. 'Come with me.'

'Elaine, at your husband's funeral, did you wink at me?'

But she merely took his hand. 'Come with me.'

He expected her to lead him upstairs to her bedroom, but to his surprise she led him outside. The night was warm; light-headed, buzzed, he was aware of the thick scent of trees and the leafy shadows on the boulevard. When she opened the car door for him, he settled into the passenger seat without speaking.

She drove out towards the university. The streets here were heavily treed, academically ivied, and deserted except for an occasional dog-walker being dragged on a leash.

Elaine Francis drove in silence.

After several blocks she pulled up in front of a mock-Tudor cottage, a quaint Shakespearean house of steep roofs, white stucco and sturdy cross-beams. On the front lawn Burton recognized a For Sale sign inscribed with the logo of Larry Francis's realty company.

'Nice place,' he said.

Elaine shut the car off and stared out the windshield. In the light of the streetlamp he glimpsed the fine cheekbones, the firm jaw. She spoke quietly. 'Every second Wednesday for six months before he died, Larry came to this house to make love to a woman who worked for his agency. Every second Wednesday I used to walk up and down over *there*,' she pointed across the street. 'Up and down, and then leave just before they came out.' Her hands lay on the steering wheel. 'You see?' she said softly. 'Don't talk to me about blue husbands. I was a blue wife.'

He moved to hold her, but she motioned him away. 'No,' she said. 'Not yet.' She withdrew the ignition key and held them up in the yellow light from the street. 'I still have the key to that house. There's no furniture in there, it's been re-carpeted and repainted. There are no buyers for it yet. Now,' she held the key in front of him, like a talisman, 'when you're ready, and when I'm ready, we'll go into that house and find an empty room, and we'll make love. But if we do, and when we do, we'll have to mean it. There'll be no winking – okay?'

And Burton – who was still a little drunk and a little nervous, but not so much so that he couldn't appreciate the colours which were suddenly exploding everywhere inside his head – nodded and said okay.

The Natural Man

Being excerpts from a diary

SEPTEMBER 14: A.M.   Morning hung like crystal, tinkle-clear and windless. Lake blemish-free, like a freshly flooded rink. Geese winging in, full of secrets. How did they ever learn that formation? (And do geese, for example, goose each other?) Fine thoughts for an idle old man, but nought else to do. Tourists all gone, leaving the world to Sakamoose and me. Bush around here feels empty now, even the bears giving up on the garbage. In two months we'll be in snow. Got to help Sakamoose with the wood, or he'll watch my white hide freeze.

P.M. Tomorrow I am seventy-seven. How does it feel, old stick? – Bit fuzzy round the edges, mum. Thoughts turn back. Forty years ago I left Jolly Old Ireland, a Jimmy Joyce gone west. What did he see through those glasses, thick as double window panes? Things I'll never glimpse, making me, Henry Fitzgibbons, the Leopold who didn't bloom. My poetry lies in the corner of our cabin, uselessly piled in our orange crate / washstand. 'To keep it off the damp floor,' I tell Sakamoose, whose eyes believe but don't understand. Art to him might be half-forgotten stories told by the elders, or dreams conjured up in the sweat lodge. 'Purity there,' I tell him. 'No fight with rhymes and metres.' 'We had no wine then,' says he. 'It made life a lot less complicated.' Sakamoose knows. A widower like me, he is nearly as old as I am, but has more wisdom. Since my retirement he has been my godfather. Like the geese, he has his secrets.

SEPTEMBER 15: A.M.   Birthday day. Weather the same, lake and sky like perfection and its mirror. Helped Sakamoose with drying fish on the beach, until he sent me away to sit on an upturned canoe. He sees what I am, an old fart gone to seed. I think he suspects my frailty will catch up with me, so he's happy to see me pretending to write. 'Crazy moony-ass poet,' he laughs of me, his exhortation of twelve years to get me to take my pen seriously. He has listened to my poetry, and has pride in it, even while I have the truth.

P.M. About noon a motor boat from the other shore came over, buzzing in the distance like a fly you can't get rid of. Conservation officer and his journalist wife. She's from England – very, very. Suspects me of being civilized because of my being born in the old country. Wants to do an article on me – The Natural Man, Thoreau, Willie Wordsworth, that kind of thing. Fishshit.

Took her to the cabin to improve her outlook. Place stinks. She picked her way around the furniture like a cat on wet grass. I wonder if she'll be able to manage a bath in a wash basin when she's seventy-seven.

Talked briefly about my work. Have I written anything? – No. Not for a dozen years. Nothing at all? – Just a diary. No, I wouldn't like to show it to anyone. Changing the subject, she sniffs through my 'library.' Very impressed, because the books are old. Sakamoose clumps around like father goose, making tea, bread and jam. He's a big man and his bulk makes me feel ineffectual. His grown-up kids whom I taught say he was that way with his wife, a woman I never knew. He still tends her grave as though it were a garden. I suppose it is.

Later at the beach, Lady Journalist tells me confidentially that she is amazed at my rapport with Sakamoose. 'Generally,' she lets me know, 'natives seem to have little sympathy for the literary mind.' Which thrills me. Now both of us are a social phenomenon.

SEPTEMBER 16: A.M.   Frost this morning, ice in the basin. Slight breeze from the north, icy-looking clouds. Sakamoose foresees an early winter. Nature told him, through the squirrels. They have never been wrong.

About 10 a.m. Lady Journalist arrives with photographer.

Candid snaps of humble lodgings, Sakamoose and I engaging in amazing rapport. Then inside for questions about childhood, nasty urban living and the Bad Old World. Sakamoose sits quietly. He has always suspected his friend of being Somebody, even when I assure him my talent is limited. He accuses me of false modesty. I cannot argue with him; after all, I have enough vanity to put up with Lady J.

Sakamoose himself is impressed with her. She sits in his chair by the stove.

P.M. Journalist and photographer leave in early evening. After a day of talking I am exhausted. Body feels older now, especially behind the eyes. Lower down, rheumatism is creeping in. Sakamoose is in high spirits, even though I explain to him that Lady Journalist receives all of the money for the article. He doesn't care. He'd feel rich if he could fix the outboard for the canoe.

SEPTEMBER 17: A.M. Morning sky speckled with dirty grey blotches. Wind from the north. Lake all ripples, fighting against one another. Geese still coming in, but fewer now.

P.M. Brief visit from Lady Journalist, takes copies of earlier poems. Will fame nuzzle this withered neck? Lady J. promises to return tomorrow. I am tired. In command now, she does all the talking. Today she took Sakamoose's chair without asking.

SEPTEMBER 18: A.M. Wind from the north colder now, sky like dull slate. Feels like snow, though some of the trees are still green. Lady Journalist and husband came for visit with government cruiser. A rough crossing they had of it, waves miniature grey mountains boiling at the peak. Lady J. will see me in three weeks, with first draft. Handshakes all round, fond farewell.

P.M. At supper Sakamoose celebrates: roast grouse, fish, bannock and canned peaches. The kettle is at the back of the stove, constantly boiling. Sakamoose keeps the fire well-stoked, knowing the heat will seep into my tightening joints. After supper we are busy, making snares, oiling traps, repairing snowshoes. The wind is really after us now, shrieking because it can't find the cracks between the logs. The plastic over the windows flutters like flags.

OCTOBER 8: A.M.   Weather turning bitterly cold. Mornings are calm, storms developing in early afternoon. Wind comes over the lake like an evil spirit.

Expect Lady J. any day now. Sakamoose keeps daily watch while he cuts last of firewood. Beach is frozen, pock-marked sand, hollows waiting for snow. Squirrels have stopped talking, so Sakamoose feels snow within two weeks. Lake should be frozen soon; ice along the margins in early morning, delicate like cob-webs, breaking with the breeze, clear-clinking Chinese wind chimes.

P.M.   At supper Sakamoose admits he is worried, growing impatient for Lady J. Have never seen him so eager. It is infectious. Even I am excited at the prospect of the article.

Lady J. had better come soon, or she will have to wait for December and solid Ski-doo ice.

OCTOBER 9: A.M.   Lake deceptively placid early this morning. Storm in the air, heavy black clouds clustering over north shore. About 9 a.m. winds picked up, trundling over the spruce to be spewed onto the lake. Built to a blizzard-like blast, changing the distant water colour, chewing up the smooth surface coming towards us. Sakamoose claimed he heard a motor boat before the storm, but by noon no sign.

P.M.   Since storm began, Sakamoose has been watching the lake. After dinner he came in, very excited. Government cruiser off-shore about one and a half miles, floundering. We went to the beach. Wind had changed direction now, howling off-shore, chopping lake into white green froth. Tiny speck of Lady J.'s boat pushed into hills and valleys of waves.

Midafternoon, Sakamoose decides to paddle out to cruiser. Apparent engine trouble gives them no progress. I try to persuade him to wait until the wind drops, but he assures me it won't. After much trouble he launches canoe, leaving me and my rheumatism on shore. Wind like ice lances, perforating my clothes.

(Suppertime and Sakamoose has not returned. Storm continues, with it the night. I went to beach and lit a signal fire, using part of the loose dock as a wind break. Tumult of wind and waves suck away even my own voice.)

I fear disaster.

OCTOBER 10: A.M.   The storm has diminished, leaving a ragged wind. At eight government cruiser put in safely, managing to stay afloat all night. In tow they had the canoe. My worst fear is realized. Sakamoose is gone.

P.M. Conservation officer organizes drag operations, but there is no body. Lady J. is appropriately sorrowful, but I have no words.

I feel I have betrayed.

OCTOBER 11: A.M.   Snow this morning out of an army blanket sky, flakes building on one another silently. Dragging is called off. I fear I will not see Sakamoose until the spring. He is hiding in the lake.

P.M. Cabin is hollow without Sakamoose's silence. Tonight I read Lady J.'s article, which she left me. Apparently I am what I appear. I am a natural man, an old hippie, forty years beyond my time. I am living in front of Walden Pond. Sakamoose is my 'native companion.'

It is not enough. For me, or for Sakamoose. I burn it.

OCTOBER 12: A.M.   Snow has put the world under a shroud.

Sakamoose, lying in cold water weeds, must approve. Already he is part of the world. In a dream I saw him as the geese, gone south for the winter, full of secrets. In spring his grave will be a garden.

P.M. I have written my first poem in twelve years.

The Shepherd's Revolt

IN THAT PART of England the hills hunch low under cloudy skies driven mad by the wind sweeping inland from the sea. Birds forced landward by the gales cackle hysterically as they wheel above the pastures and open fields. Below them the sheep graze, as much a part of the landscape as the stone fences, the hedgerows, or the cottages themselves. Here the land has been cultivated for centuries; even as the boulders at Stonehenge were being raised on the plain, men ploughed and planted these fields. Their marks are still here – long, low ridges of tufted grass, etched like scars across the hill's face. As old as those scars are the pathways of the sheep, and as old as the sheep is the knowledge of the men who tend them.

From the road that runs along the top of the downs you can see the farm flattened out beneath you, the steepness of the hills curiously levelled by perspective. The red brick manor house flashes among the trees where narrow lanes twist and wind up to the sheep paddocks, to the grey row of workers' cottages, and to the hay barn, beside which the lambing pens have been built this year.

The coops, constructed of straw bales lashed together and gated at the open end by woven wattle hurdles, look like a row of straw-walled caves strung out neatly, side by side. In front of them the holding pens have been littered with straw and bound in by extra strands of barbed wire as protection for the ewes and newborn lambs they will enclose. The whole resembles a miniature sunlit village surrounded by green.

In the distance you can see the shepherd arrive on a small blue tractor. He is an old man who stiffly dismounts his vehicle and bends cautiously to pat the black-and-white speck that is his dog.

The sheep move unhurriedly towards the gate at the corner of the field nearest the lambing pens. Now and then you hear the shepherd's whistle shrill above the sound of the wind. The man directs his dog slowly and precisely. He has been a shepherd most of his life and has the reputation of being a good worker, a wise, gentle man. A bachelor, he lives with his dog Kip in the cottage at the base of Folson's Pike. His name is Bert Williams, and he is ill. Look: as you watch, his tiny figure stumbles ... stumbles and falls, face down on the hillside. Against the green pasture his body stretches into a thin black line.

After a while nothing moves except the wind over the grass, and the black-and-white speck, which dashes frantically around him.

'BLOODY HELL.' Colonel Oldham-Ramsell drummed his fingers on the idling Land Rover's steering wheel and peered down the road for a sign of Arthur's car. 'Bloody damned hell.'

He thought again of the funeral. A dismal affair. Poor Bert. To be buried in the rain. And Kip making all that row. At the graveside, the cook, Mrs Macklery, had cried uncontrollably, until the minister actually paused in his address to lay a comforting arm around her burly shoulders. Arthur had stood, cap off and head bowed to the grey drizzle; even Moffat, the sideburned tractor driver, had stifled a sniffle. They had all been fond of the old shepherd. Losing him had been like losing a member of the family.

Colonel Oldham switched off the engine. In the silence the wind moaned against the car. He stared across the heath at the lambing pens. Three thousand expectant ewes, God knows how many of them requiring a shepherd's experienced hand and eye to bring them fat and healthy to market – the loss of the shepherd was tragic and confusing, and yet absurd, too. In spite of food supplements, chemical fertilizers and the latest farm machinery, Oldham Grange still relied on the old ways for survival. One man, a shepherd, could make the difference between prosperity and failure. One man.

'Bloody hell.'

Whining, Arthur's car appeared at the bottom of the slope and slowly crawled up the narrow road. When it reached the gate leading into the top paddock, it stopped and Arthur got out.

'Well?' Colonel Oldham rolled down his window.

Bandy-legged and wiry, the farm manager took off his cap and scratched his head. 'I been all round, sir, and they all be engaged. Them as weren't busy now 'spect they will be shortly. 'Enry Wallace of Breckleburn farm reckons as 'e might like to shepherd full time for you, but only arter lambing's completed.'

'Has a contract, has he?'

''E does, sir, and shearing for wages. And 'e gets the cottage year round, rates and all.'

'Yes. Well, we can match that. But is there no one available in the mean time? What about young Thomas?'

'Away 't agricultural college. I expect it could be left to I to watch over lambing in't arternoons, sir. But it be a night man we need.'

'Yes.' Colonel Oldham rubbed at a smudge on the windshield. 'Well then, Arthur, you continue your inquiries and I'll have Lucy post an advert in the *Exchange*. The rush of lambs hasn't begun yet, has it?'

'Not yet, sir.'

'Good. Then we still have time. Not to worry.'

But driving home, Colonel Oldham inadvertently ground the gears. These days shepherds were in short supply. In a world of computers and unionized farm labourers, shepherds had all but disappeared. The local labour exchange had laughed at his inquiries. 'Shepherds, Colonel Oldham? No demand for shepherds until the Christmas pageant, I'm afraid.' Chortling, as though Oldham Grange were some quaint monument to the past.

It *was* a monument to the past; but it was a modern farm too. Colonel Oldham had struck a delicate balance between the past and the present. He sometimes thought of the farm as a living body, its bones set down in the earth itself, its blood the stoop and lift of successive generations.

He steered the Land Rover between hedgerows that had been planted at the time of Shakespeare. Past and Present. Let the cynics laugh. Come Christmas they'd still want their racks of lamb. They too were creatures of tradition.

But I'm going to have to hire *someone,* Colonel Oldham thought.

As soon as I saw the ad in the paper I knew I had no choice: six weeks' work for £400. In those days, in England, that was good money. I figured my luck had finally changed. The wages I'd earned in New Zealand had run out and the original money I'd left Canada with was long gone. Even with a work visa I'd been having a hard time making ends meet in England; the height of my working career there had been in London where I delivered false teeth for a dental supply company. Then that ad jumped up and hit me in the face: sheep. And in that part of England. It was more than a coincidence, it was an omen or something. If Granddad had been around, he would've laughed. He'd been born somewhere down in that Wessex country. There might even have been some Hendershots still living around there.

This colonel who advertised was asking an eighteen-hour day, but that didn't mean he wouldn't let me eat or sleep, and that's all I needed just then. Forty winks and a couple of steaks. That and enough money to buy a ticket to some place sunny. Spain or some place. I was still running then. I could still see Granddad like he was at the end, as skinny as a bag of sticks. I'd run from his funeral, run from the bank that foreclosed on the farm, run halfway around the world, and here I was — right back where he'd started. In all the years I'd lived with Granddad he never stopped talking about 'the old country.' But I could never figure out what it really meant to him. If the old country was so great, why'd he ever leave it? Or if it had been so bad that he'd had to leave it, why'd he always talk about it as if it was the place where he belonged? Why did I sometimes think it was the place where I belonged? I couldn't figure it all out.

But that job was crying for me. 'Wanted immediately.' So I phoned, and caught the next bus to Longbridge Downs.

The village was a cluster of stone cottages, some of them with thatched roofs, a few farm buildings and a post office, a pub and a gas station. It was hunkered in the folds of those long rolling hills that the people there call 'downs.' It was real sheep country: the ground was a bit rocky, sprinkled with chips of flint, but it was clean land, and even that early in the year – March – the grass was shaping up thick and sweet. The air smelled fresh, and the ewes stood out on the hills like snowflakes on a pool table. After the bus dropped me off I walked around for a while, taking it all in. Then I asked the garage man the way to Oldham Grange.

'WHAT DID YOU SAY his name was?' By his own admission, Colonel Oldham was bad with names.

"Endershot, sir. Canadian 'e be, though. 'E do say 'is family originated somewhere near Salisbury.'

'Um. I hope he's had experience.'

"E says 'e and 'is grandfather raised sheep in Canada. And 'e 'as a letter from a Mr Burgess in Gisborne, New Zealand, and another from a gentleman in New South Wales. 'E do come recommended, sir. 'E be well travelled about, as I judge.'

'I should say so. You showed him round, did you? And how did he seem?'

"E seemed right enough to me, sir. 'E do know 'is sheep, I will say. We looked in't far end of steadin', and 'e noticed one of the blackfaces with calcium deficiency. 'E popped right over the fence and tipped 'er up, no bother, sir. Checked the old girl for eye response and lambing and all. 'E seemed efficient enough. Gentle, as well.'

'Do you think he'll be able to put in the hours required?'

"E looks strong enough. Bit on the lean side, but a worker, all the same.'

'Yes. Well ... put him on then, Arthur. Have him come round to the office when you've got him settled, before you take him up to the lambing pens. And make sure Moffat has transported that barley cake up to the lambing shed. Oh, and you might inform Mrs Macklery that Master ... Hendershot will be taking his meals in the kitchen. She can arrange meal times with him.'

'Right sir.'

The first time I met Colonel Oldham he was standing in his office in front of a shelf of trophies. He was a tall, white-haired old man, probably in his mid-seventies. He had a military backbone though I understood he'd been retired from the army for almost twenty years. His face was long, his shoulders cramped. I could imagine him in the old days with a swagger stick under one arm, barking orders. Not that he ever barked at me, or any of the other workers — at least not that I ever saw. He was a dignified man, very straightforward. He told you what he thought. I didn't hold that against him. I still don't.

'Master Hendershot,' he said, and shook my hand. Master. He said it once, like it was a joke, and he never called me 'Master' again. In a way he was warning me: there was only one master here — him.

He told me about my duties, which were pretty much what I expected. I was to live in the shepherd's hut and perform the difficult deliveries, feed the sickly lambs, match lambs with their mothers, ring tails and testicles, number the twins and triplets — all things I'd done before but, as the Colonel pointed out, probably never under so much pressure. 'My shepherd has a hand in every aspect of lambing here,' he said. 'Labour intensive. I provide a bonus should you exceed the one hundred and fifty per cent production quota. From my three thousand ewes, I expect forty-five hundred lambs. My labourers will help with the feeding, of course, and shifting the sheep to the various paddocks. I shall rely on you, however, to attend to the everyday details of the job.'

Then we chatted for a while. He mentioned Canada and a trip he'd made to the Arctic. I told him about Granddad. 'The name should ring a bell,' the Colonel said, 'but I can't place it. I suspect your grandfather was a bit before my time.'

'He emigrated when he was twelve. He was eighty-three when he died.'

'Ah.'

I asked him about his trophies — cups, and horses mounted in silver. He said he'd won them in equestrian events, years ago. 'I only ride for pleasure now, however. And the hunt, of course.'

'Fox hunts?'

'We have a number of foxes around here.'

'Real foxes? I thought that wasn't allowed any more. Granddad said they used drags for the hunt.'

'In most ordinary circumstances we do. It just so happens that once a season we ... accidentally come across the real thing.'

He smiled. His eyes were a washed-out blue, the colour of rainwater in a jar. He wasn't unfriendly, just factual. I could see him leading a crowd of tally-ho-ers over fences and through ditches.

'Back home in Saskatchewan when we had trouble with coyotes, we found a rifle was handy.'

'You will find, Hendershot, that this is not home.'

I didn't know what to say to that. Something hung there between us. "This is not home." Okay. I could buy that. But something grabbed me by the throat. It's hard to explain now, but for a minute there, with the Colonel, I felt like I was going to fall off something. It wasn't only his mention of the fox hunt, it was something else. It was like ... it was like the time I climbed my first castle over there. I climbed up these steps that had grooves worn in them from all the feet that had gone up them before. And then I came out on this parapet, with the wind howling around me, and I poked my head through one of those crenellations in the wall, and I looked down. But I didn't feel like a guy who should be on a castle wall. I tried to imagine wearing a suit of mail and carrying the latest Norman crossbow – but I couldn't do it. I figured that if I'd been alive in those days, I would've been one of those hairy guys down below who was trying to climb up the wall. I mean, you can call it peasant attitude or anything you want – but that's how I felt.

RISING in his stirrups, Colonel Oldham steadied himself with one hand in the gelding's grey mane. The horse snorted and took a half-step forward, lowering its head against the taut reins for a chance to crop the grass.

'That's him down there,' the Colonel told his daughter, who was astride the mare. Lucy squinted at the orange-and-blue blur she knew must be the tractor and cart.

'I don't have my lenses in,' she said.

'We'll move closer.' Her father urged Romulus with his knees. 'He's picking up a ewe.'

The two horses ambled down the grassy slope, their rumps rolling with the slow pace and angle of descent. Around them the sheep moved shyly away. Thirty yards from the tractor the horses stopped.

The cart's tailgate had been lowered, and Hendershot was tempting a ewe to enter it by dragging her newborn lamb in front of her. In spite of the wind, the riders could hear the shepherd's voice as he crept backwards to the waiting cart. 'Come on, mum.' He spoke in a soothing monotone, holding the wet wriggling lamb by the rear leg until its bleats attracted the wandering mother who trotted this way and that, head up and bleating distractedly. When the lamb was silent and the mother lost sight of it, the shepherd imitated the youngster's complaints. 'Maaa-aaa, maaa-aaa –' until the ewe renewed her faith in the pursuit by sniffing and licking the head of her captured lamb.

At last Hendershot enticed the ewe into the cart and closed the tailgate.

'I say,' Colonel Oldham approached. 'That was quite a performance.'

'Thanks.'

'I expect it was necessary.'

'They talk to me, so I talk to them.'

'Quite,' the Colonel said doubtfully. He twisted in the saddle and introduced his daughter. 'Hendershot's grandfather emigrated from this region – about the turn of the century, Hendershot?'

'Nineteen-ten.'

'Nineteen-ten.' The Colonel nodded. 'Remarkable coincidence.'

'Have you any relations living hereabouts?' Lucy Oldham, married to a television executive, knew what it was to show an interest in people.

'I haven't found any so far. At least none that want to claim me.'

'How are you getting on here, then?' Colonel Oldham interrupted.

'I'm keeping up to things.'

'How many ewes delivered last night?'

'About twenty.'

'And what percentage of those were twins, would you say?'

'About half. And one set of triplets. All the rest were singles.'

'Did you lose any?'

'No, none.'

'Good, good.' Colonel Oldham turned to his daughter. 'Very promising start.'

'I suppose it is,' she said.

Colonel Oldham gathered up his reins. 'Well, keep up the good work, Hendershot. By the way, I noticed a ewe at the top of the paddock there; nearly due, I should think.'

'I haven't been up there yet. Thanks.'

'You will see to her, though, won't you?'

'Right away.'

'Because at Christmas market we'll likely get fifteen pounds for fat lamb.'

'That's a lot of money.'

'It certainly makes each lamb precious, doesn't it?'

The horses trotted daintily away, leaving the shepherd to watch them follow the fence to the lower gate. Striding toward the tractor, Hendershot ruffled the ewe's ears and grinned. 'Home on the range, big mama.'

The ewe stopped licking her lamb to look inquiringly over the cart's side.

That lamb at the top of the field came out of the womb headfirst and forelegs outstretched like a diver off a springboard. He was covered in a clear bag of slime speckled with blood, and his hooves were yellow and soft at the tips. His long ears were laid back like a jackrabbit who's trying to outsprint a car. I laid him near his mother's head and she started to lick him right away. The bag peeled off his head like wet plastic. I propped his mouth open and gave his head a shake until he sucked my

*finger. In a few minutes he sat up, ears drooping as if he'd just woke up
from a sleep in the rain. The ewe talked to him in her nuzzle language
and he tried to answer her. Before he was dry he'd had his first drink
and was teetering on four long skinny legs.*

*I delivered hundreds of lambs like him. Those were the ones I liked
to see. Those were the healthy ones.*

'LUCY?'

'What is it *now*, Daddy?'

'All the invitations have been answered, haven't they? There
isn't anyone we've left out?'

'I made sure of that weeks ago. Really, you fret too much.
Look at you. Why don't you go along to bed?'

'I expect you're right. Oh – Mrs Macklery knows about the
stirrup cup recipe, doesn't she? You know, the one your mother
used to insist on?'

'Mrs Macklery has everything planned, Daddy – right down
to fresh nutmeg for the punch and oysters on order for the steak
and kidney pie. Really, we went through all this *weeks* ago.'

'I just want to be certain, that's all.'

'Well, you needn't fret. And anyway, I thought you weren't
going to indulge in nostalgia this time.'

'Since when has hospitality become nostalgia?'

'Since you've decided you're old, Daddy.'

'I *am* old.'

'Not nearly as old as some. You do look tired though. I really
think you ought to let Arthur do more – it is his job, after all.'

'Arthur's been busy with the hay merchant just now. At any
rate, the lambing gives me an excuse to exercise Romulus.'

'Rodney can exercise Romulus. You should be getting some
rest. Go along now. I'm just going to watch the news. John's
helped devise the new format and he wants an "unbiased opinion
from the provinces".'

'Will John be down for the weekend?'

'If he can. If not, I promised I'd go up to London for a few
days.'

'All right. But you *will* be back in time for the hunt.'
'I'll be back for the hunt, Daddy. Go along to bed now.'
'All right, dear. Goodnight, then.'
'Good*night*, Daddy.'

AT NIGHT the shepherd herds the ewes into the lambing pens where they curl up like mounds of snow in the darkness. If you or the Colonel were to go out, and if the wind were to draw the clouds away from the moon, you could stand at the top of the paddock and see directly across the downs. The lambing pens are momentarily awash in moonlight, highlighted like the negative of a film.

The shepherd's hut lists at a slight angle to the hillside and throws a yellow patch of light from its window. At irregular intervals the door to the hut opens, and a bobbing flashlight leads the shepherd's feet through a series of gates into the lambing pens. The sheep lift their heads and stare into the light beam; some of them grunt to their feet, puffing breaths of steam. The shepherd moves stealthily through the flock, crooning snatches of cowboy songs. Occasionally the circle of light discovers a new lamb, lingers on the shivering form, then slides among the ewes in search of the mother. When the ewes and their newborn lambs are locked in their coops, the light threads its way back to the shepherd's hut. Later it reappears as the shepherd patrols the coops and nursery pens, feeding warm milk from an oversized bottle to those lambs he considers weak or sickly.

In time the clouds obscure the moon. A light drizzle falls, as fine and insistent as mist. The flashlight bobs and flickers, wanders through the pens and around them, through the pens and around them, until at last the sky dissolves into a pale grey, and the flashlight disappears at the rising of the sun.

Just before dawn that day I came across a ewe in the paddock with her lamb half-delivered. His swollen head hung out of her womb like a dead thing while she grazed. Every time I moved toward her, she shied away. Finally I had to drive alongside her with the tractor, jump off and bulldog her to the ground. I throttled the tractor down and shut off the key before I jumped, but while I had the ewe pinned down the tractor kept rolling. It was aimed at the barn, gathering speed, like something out of the Keystone Cops. So I sprinted after it. I let go of the ewe, kicked off my rubber boots and tore down the hill in my socks. I had to jump into the trailer and crawl up over the hitch. I banged my head on the roll-bar and was shaking by the time I got the thing stopped.

I sat there in the half-light sweating and listening for my Granddad's laugh. I knew what he would've said: If you wanted to ride, what did you get off for in the first place?

By the time I captured the ewe again the sun was rising. A foreleg was holding her lamb back, but once that was free he popped out like a wet fish. He was okay, but he was only the first of triplets. The other two in there were tied together like a Chinese puzzle. I laid the ewe in the trailer, rolled up my sleeve and reached deep inside her. I lay on my stomach and looked at the sky, as if it could help me sort out the legs and the heads. The ewe strained, I pulled. My fingers cramped up. My hand was a blind man.

The ewe worked hard for over an hour – pushed and strained, and let out bleats of pure pain. 'Come on, mum,' I urged her. 'Come on.' In the end she delivered the two other lambs, each smaller than the last. When I put them near her muzzle she was too exhausted to lick them. So I rubbed them down with straw. Then I checked the four of them over. The last two lambs were barely alive. The ewe's eyes were glazed and her breathing was shallow. Her tongue lolled out of her mouth.

I put the lambs on her teats and squeezed as much colostrum into them as I could. Then I gave the mother penicillin and calcium. I talked to her, and once she lifted her head. By the time I got her back to the coops, though, she was dead.

I lost two ewes that way, then another from old age. And once I found an old ewe who'd slipped between the stone slabs of the old Roman road that lay hidden in the gorse. She'd broken both her forelegs, so I had to put her down. The crows led me to her; they'd pecked the eyes out of her newborn lamb.

Seeing all those carcasses together, I remembered the day the stock trucks leased by the bank drove into the yard and loaded up what was left of Granddad's flock. Those sheep weren't killed, of course, but it was a kind of slaughter all the same. We watched from the porch, both of us feeling useless – Granddad because he was sick, and me because I figured I hadn't worked hard enough. Seeing the Colonel's dead sheep gave me the same feeling I'd had about the ones Granddad and I had lost.

It was like the whole thing was happening again.

'RIGHT THEN, MATE?' Having escaped his duties at the horse stables, Rodney leaned over the hurdle and craned his thin neck into the coop where Hendershot examined a ewe. The shepherd was pushing what looked like bloody bread dough into the sheep's womb. 'Christ, what that might be?'

'A prolapse. Her womb's come out. Hand me that retainer, would you?'

Rodney passed over a plastic device that looked like a yawning w. Hendershot dipped it in a bucket of soapy antiseptic, then inserted the contraption, tying the forks to the sheep's wool. 'That ought hold you, mum.' He wiped his hands on the ewe's back. The ewe lay on her side, panting, her yellow eyes fringed by coarse white lashes.

'I think she's carrying twins,' Hendershot said. 'We'll have to keep an eye on her.' He stepped out of the coop and started back along the muddy alley towards the shepherd's hut.

'Ooyy!'

Hendershot turned to Rodney. 'What's up?'

Rodney jerked his thumb to the far end of the coops. 'It be the Colonel.' He ducked his head and busied himself with fastening a hurdle gate more securely.

Colonel Oldham trudged towards them, clumsy in his rubber boots, which smacked in the sucking mud. He carried a dead lamb in one hand. 'I found him in behind the barn,' the Colonel said. He laid the lamb at his feet. One side of the animal's throat and abdomen had been torn away; the ribs gaped nakedly, gutted.

'Fox,' Hendershot said.

'Yes.' The Colonel spoke with a certain sadness. 'I thought there might be some about.' He looked the shepherd in the eye. 'A bit of a quandary, this. I shouldn't like to lose too many lambs to the fox – but neither should I like to lose the fox.' He nudged the corpse with his boot. 'I've instructed Arthur to surround the lambing pens with creosote-treated twine. He and the labourers should be at it today.' Colonel Oldham detected the shepherd's scepticism. 'It's a tried and proven measure, Hendershot.'

'I bet it is.'

'And you needn't concern yourself with the loss of this little chap. Any lamb lost to foxes will not be included in our bargain.'

The shepherd shrugged. 'It seems like a waste, that's all.'

The Colonel nodded. 'It's one of those paradoxical prices that one has to pay.'

Hendershot squatted next to the stiffened lamb and peered. 'Fox couldn't have been too hungry,' he said. 'All he ate was the liver, some of the stomach.' He glanced up. 'But I'd feel better if I had a rifle.'

'Not necessary.'

'I'm not saying I'd use it.'

'Then why would you want it?'

The shepherd stood. 'Maybe it's one of those paradoxical prices one has to pay.'

If the Colonel's face hadn't been already red, he might've flushed. At the hurdle, Rodney strangled a giggle, which came out, convincingly enough, a cough.

'If you have something to say, Hendershot, by all means say it.'

The shepherd wiped his hands on his jeans. 'For what it's worth, I think this fox hunt business is bullshit. I don't see the point of it.'

The Colonel nodded. 'I can understand that – though I see no need to be vulgar about it.' The Colonel fisted his hands in his duffle coat pockets. He lifted his chin, as though listening to a sound far away. 'Are you a conservationist, Hendershot?'

'Not really. Right now, I'm a shepherd, that's all.'

'And one I'd like to keep on until the contract's finished.'

'Are you saying I'm going to get fired?'

'I'm saying that I am your employer. Ultimately the running of this farm, its success or failure – its lambs *and* foxes for that matter – is my responsibility. Just as it is my responsibility to pay your wages. I think you understand that, don't you?'

Hendershot looked at his feet in the mud. Finally he bent and picked up the dead lamb.

'I understand that. But I want to go on record as requesting that you keep *your* foxes away from *my* lambs.'

The Colonel smiled thinly. '*My* lambs,' he corrected. 'But – fair enough. It can be done.'

The shepherd merely nodded.

A ewe recognizes her own lamb by scent: she can smell part of herself on him. Unless he's dead or been separated from her too long, a ewe'll do everything to make her lamb comfortable. She'll shelter him from the cold, let him suck when he's hungry, nuzzle him when he's lonely or feels like conversation. I've seen a lamb curl up on his mother's back, lie in the sun and whisper secrets in her ear.

But sometimes I get a lamb nobody wants because he's weak or is taken for dead, or I made a mistake and separated him from his mother for so long he's coated himself with some other smell. Then I've got to mother him onto a ewe that's got no lamb. Most times that isn't easy. When a ewe finds herself with a strange lamb she'll butt him, kick him, and generally make his life miserable. I have to tie her up, hobble her – maybe tie a hind leg back. Then if the lamb doesn't give up trying to feed himself, in a week or so the ewe will learn to accept him, and finally come to consider him her own.

Now when that happens I feel proud of myself. I've been master of the situation – changed something. I even think I've bent that ewe's will to my own. But see, it doesn't work that way. When that ewe is first tied up she stands trembling with her ears laid back, and actually flinches when the lamb sucks the teat. While I'm there she puts up with him like he is a job or a punishment. But tied up in that coop with that lamb twenty-four hours a day, she softens. MOTHER *is in her guts.*

Tying her up only gives her a chance to feel what she wants to feel in the first place. What her giving birth and being a sheep like a thousand years' worth of sheep forces her to feel: to be a mother.

More than anything else she'll work to keep that lamb alive. It's in her nature, that's all.

THE WET SNOW falls silently. Large flakes drift out of the night sky, smoothing the downs into a muted luminescence, as though the dark grass had just this moment died and blanched in the passing. Listen: the stillness weighs heavily ... listen: the flakes are as audible as breath as they build on one another, rounding out the curve of this hill and that one ... softening the line of roof tiles, once red ... burying the thrusting grass ...

The falling snow thickens and dilutes the darkness to an opaque grey. From his study window Colonel Oldham peers out through cupped hands and sweating glass. The snow obliterates everything: even the oaks along the lane are invisible. Really, he thinks, the seasons have run amok in recent years: that terrible heat in October, now snow in April ...

There are times when Colonel Oldham feels almost dithery.

He returns to the window. A sudden eddy has set the flakes swirling.

He really should have a fire put on in here.

THE MORNING AFTER the storm Colonel Oldham walked through the new white world and complained to Arthur, his manager, that it looked as though the shepherd slept all night. A patrol of the coops had yielded several lambs dead of exposure.

'Twelve lambs lost, Arthur,' the Colonel said, gesturing with his walking stick. 'Each slack-bellied and hollow. Unfed, it appears to me.' Arthur followed the Colonel a pace or two behind – perhaps out of obsequiousness – but possibly out of mere shortness of stride. The sun and dazzling snow had enervated Colonel Oldham; his previous night's worries lay subdued before him like the snow, clean and uncomplicated. He strode along optimistic and determined, and only stopped when he reached the shepherd's hut. 'Get him up, then, Arthur.'

Arthur climbed the steps and knocked on the dutch doors. There was no answer. He opened the door and peered inside. ''E's not in.'

'Over here.' Hendershot's head appeared around the side of the hut. He was lowering a lamb's corpse into a large gunny sack, which when full would be shipped off to the knacker's, ultimately to become dog food. Bleary-eyed and unshaven, the shepherd gave every impression of a man close to exhaustion. 'Hell of a night,' he said by way of explanation. 'The weather seemed to affect the ewes – I had over eighty deliveries last night.'

'And a dozen losses as well,' Colonel Oldham pointed out.

'A dozen? I didn't think there'd be that many. I did miss a bottle feeding of the ones at the far end last night. You sure there's a dozen?'

'A dozen.' The Colonel leaned on his walking stick. 'I suspect you missed more than one feeding, Hendershot.'

The shepherd cocked his head to one side. 'Is that so?' He nodded to the farm manager. 'How about you, Arthur? You think I missed more than one feeding?'

Arthur ducked his head. 'Them lambs be 'ollow, mate.'

'Aw shit.' Hendershot squatted to secure the burlap bag with a length of orange twine. He pulled at the twine viciously, as one man would garrotte another. His hand slipped, and he skinned his knuckle against the hut wall. Blood oozed into the wound, beaded, and dripped into the snow. Hendershot glanced at the cut as if it belonged to someone else.

'I built a shelter out of bales in the hay barn last night,' he said. 'I took most of the ewes and lambs out of the coops and herded them all in there. Apparently I missed some.'

'Apparently.'

'Look, obviously you're not happy with the job I'm doing here. Maybe I ought to leave.'

The Colonel frowned quizzically. 'Without pay?'

'I'm willing to forgo the bonus.'

'I wasn't talking about the bonus.'

The shepherd stood, running his hands through his already unruly hair. 'Let me get this straight. If I leave now, I don't get paid?'

The Colonel shrugged. 'You signed a contract for the lambing.'

'There was no final date on it that I could see.'

'There rarely is. The precise date of the end of the lambing is usually left to the discretion of the owner of the sheep – and to the sheep themselves, of course.'

For confirmation Hendershot looked at Arthur, who nodded.

'Jesus Christ.' Hendershot paced in a small circle. 'Jesus Christ.' He stopped. 'I don't get it. You'll have to excuse me, maybe I'm stupid – but I don't get it. According to you I'm not doing the job right. I want to leave, but you still want me to stay. Why?'

'I need a shepherd. There are none to be had.'

'So I'm your last resort.'

'And I yours.'

Unhappy, but nevertheless appreciative of the Colonel's accuracy, the shepherd shook his head. 'Okay. But I want a quitting date. Something exact. I'm giving you my notice. Two weeks from today.'

'The day of the hunt. Good. You can stay until the hunt is over and most of my guests have eaten – which should put us at seven in the evening, I should think. You'll be able to pick up your pay packet from Arthur then.'

'Good enough.'

However tentatively, the two men shook hands.

I didn't see much of the Colonel after I'd given him my notice. He was too busy, and I was too. I became cold about the whole business. I delivered the lambs, moved them from one paddock to another, taught Rod how to back up a tractor with a trailer hitched to it. I relaxed in the rhythm of the job – probably because I knew it would be over soon. For the first time in over a year I started making plans. I'd go to Spain for a couple of weeks, get a tan and maybe meet a Spanish girl. I'd drink vino tinto and make love on the beach. Then I'd fly back home and look for a different line of work – maybe I'd even go to university. Sheep and farms I'd leave behind forever. I'd had enough of them.

Once I went into Salisbury to look at the cathedral and go through the church records. It turned out Granddad was the last of the English Hendershots: none survived him. On my way out the beadle reminded me that the cathedral was sinking into the soft Salisbury soil, so I threw some money into the donations box. But it seemed right to me that the cathedral and the Hendershots should disappear from that country. It felt right.

Most of the time I spent on the job. The snow melted and the days grew warmer. I had a chance to rest some days; I slept on the bunk at the far end of the shepherd's hut, under the medicine shelf. Rod watched over the sheep in the afternoons. He hadn't had much experience with sheep, being still in high school. But he was a fast learner, good with animals, and I found we could split the work almost down the middle. The rush of lambs eased up, and according to Arthur we were headed for a bonus. Things were going well.

Then the day before the hunt I saw a ewe who thought her lamb was lost. She bleated all over a twenty-acre paddock looking for him, while he followed her, bawling desperately. She looked stupid and exasperating, but there wasn't much I could do about it. Her instinct dragged her wherever it wanted to go.

I followed her in the tractor. I cursed her because her lamb was having a hard time keeping up. I wanted to get them both into the cart and back to the coop. I figured the ewe was being stubborn, and ignorant. Finally she wandered into the angle formed by the fence, where I caught her.

It wasn't until after I got her in the cart that I found the other lamb. He lay cold and stiff in the tall grass along the fence. He'd been dead a long time.

She must have had him hours before she delivered the second one. When I put the corpse in the cart she tried to nuzzle it back to life.

I should have realized then. My grandfather had always claimed that animals – even sheep – can teach us things. I should have recognized that in her own way the ewe was trying to tell me something.

THE EARLY MORNING MIST dissipates so gradually you are scarcely aware of the process. One moment the trees are ghosts floating in a grey veil; the next they stand out solidly against the green downs.

In the courtyard the hounds strain at their leads, yelping and whining in anticipation. Riders and their grooms make redundant last-minute checks on bridles, cinches and stirrup lengths. Ladies secure their hair under black riding helmets. Leather creaks under weight, metal rings on metal. Conversation is limited to spirited jokes and nervous laughter.

Leading the riders Colonel Oldham sits astride his grey gelding and leans, soldier-fashion, to give the nodding houndsman last-minute instructions. The riders lapse into silence, their horses skitter and shy on the cobblestones, and just when the smell of the horses and leather and dung seem the distasteful tangibility of an unbearable delay – the houndsman's horn sounds, and they canter away between the farm buildings, wheel around the open gate and into the lane. Across the pasture the riders post on bent knees, then lean forward eagerly as their mounts stretch into a gallop.

Throughout the day you glimpse the hunters – now strung out along a hill's slope, now bunched as they near a hedge jump. Around trees, over hedges; slowing to a walk to cross a paved thoroughfare, charging recklessly across open fields. Somewhere ahead the hounds clamour their deep-throated excitement; somewhere ahead of them the fox lopes among the gorse.

From a distance you watch the horses leap the fence into the top paddock; the sheep scatter before them like white tumbleweeds. The lambs sprint and stumble on knobby forelegs, or stand vacantly as the riders surge toward, ride over, rumble past them. Near the hut you see the shepherd running clumsily, comically across the downs. He is waving his arms and must be shouting, but his voice, like the horses' hooves, thuds like a dull thing against the hills – like a stone falling to soft ground.

The riders canter along the fence and enter the lane through the gate.

The shepherd stands motionless in the valley and watches them disappear. The trodden lambs are strewn like rags in the field. A slight wind rolls over the field in waves and ruffles their fleeces. The grass, in waves, laps around the shepherd's feet.

Nine dead lambs. That wasn't so many. They probably didn't spoil the average. And their being dead ... well, that's where they wound up anyway. They were born, they got fat, and then they were lamb chops.

But I said to hell with it. That day was my last on the job, so what did it matter? I went back into the hut and waited for seven o'clock. Rod herded the ewes back into the pens. I sat there. When they hollered for it, I bottle-fed the lambs behind the stove.

I lay on the bunk, watched the night come on. I heard Rod get his bicycle. He was in no mood to talk either. He just said he was going to get some supper. The darkness came down like a big black bird. The coal in the grate glowed red. I could hear the ewes outside grunting and chewing their cud. The lambs in the pens bleated for milk and the ewes in the paddock answered, thinking those were the lambs they'd lost.

I lay brooding in the hut and waited for time to pass. Six o'clock; six-fifteen; six-thirty. All my gear was packed; I was ready to go. I pumped up the lantern until the mantle glowed white, as if I needed it to gather my words. I wasn't much for talking, but I rehearsed what I'd tell the Colonel when I went to collect my wages. I imagined the different ways I'd deliver my judgement – to him alone in his office, or in the hall in front of his daughter, or better yet in the dining room in front of his guests. Oh, I'd tell him – I'd tell them all. I'd march in with the wind while his guests were still seated at the table, I wouldn't even take off my sheep-shitted boots. I'd pronounce him – all of them – dead. As dead as their castles and sinking cathedrals, as dead as their faces filled with their stuffy dead food – as dead as the shepherd whose raincoat still hung on a nail near the door –

I was well worked up when I heard it. It's a bleat, but not quite;

more like a cry. A ewe will hold her breath and strain to deliver a lamb. And when he won't come, the pain is forced out in a hollow sound.

It was the prolapse, and her time was due. Her time was due, see, so I got up. I took the old raincoat to kneel on, and a can of lambing oil to keep the womb moist. I took a syringe, a bottle of penicillin, and some calcium, just in case.

Oh, I swore a bit. I cursed and waved my arms, but there wasn't much in it. Because the instant that bleat touched my ear, all that fine hot air went out of me and left me empty except for one thing – the thing I'd never thought of before: I knew the difference between men like the Colonel and me. And though I could argue that the difference is money or class or tradition or country or upbringing, or a hundred other things, I don't think it's anything like that. It's a difference inside, that's all.

Just a difference, and I couldn't fight it because it was probably older and a damn sight deeper than I'd ever imagined. All the talk in the world wasn't going to change it. I sure couldn't change it. I'd probably have to buy back my grandfather's farm and work it the rest of my life before I'd understand what was going on.

I looked at my watch: seven o'clock. Officially I was laid off. But I picked up the flashlight and the lambing medicines and stepped outside. The prolapse was bleating in the dark.

As I walked toward her it was the feeling of pride, more than anything else, that took me by surprise.

DON DICKINSON was born in 1947 in Prince Albert. He graduated from the University of Saskatchewan in 1970. For the next seven years he travelled widely, working at jobs as varied as labourer, fitness instructor, and shepherd. In 1979 he received an MFA in creative writing from the University of British Columbia. While at UBC, he was fiction editor of *Prism International.* He now teaches in a high school in Lillooet, B.C. and is working on a novel.